Alfred Russel Wallace

Bad Times

an essay on the present depression of trade

Alfred Russel Wallace

Bad Times

an essay on the present depression of trade

ISBN/EAN: 9783337400187

Printed in Europe, USA, Canada, Australia, Japan

Cover: Foto ©Andreas Hilbeck / pixelio.de

More available books at **www.hansebooks.com**

BAD TIMES:

AN ESSAY ON THE PRESENT DEPRESSION OF TRADE,
TRACING IT TO ITS SOURCES IN ENORMOUS FOREIGN
LOANS, EXCESSIVE WAR EXPENDITURE, THE INCREASE
OF SPECULATION AND OF MILLIONAIRES, AND THE
DEPOPULATION OF THE RURAL DISTRICTS;
WITH SUGGESTED REMEDIES.

BY

ALFRED RUSSEL WALLACE, LL.D.

"In regretting the depopulation of the country I inveigh against the
increase of our luxuries; and here too I expect the shout of
modern politicians against me."
GOLDSMITH, *Dedication to Deserted Village.*

London:

MACMILLAN AND CO.

1885

Richard Clay and Sons,
BREAD STREET HILL, LONDON, E.C.,
and Bungay, Suffolk.

PREFACE.

THE present work was written last March, in competition for the Pears prize of one hundred guineas for the best essay on the present depression of trade. It did not obtain the prize, and it is therefore now submitted to the judgment of the public—and more especially of the working classes, with some additional matter in the earlier chapters which could not be compressed within the limits assigned to the competing essays.

As our existing land-system in its relation to depression of trade is somewhat fully treated in the following pages, this seems the proper place to state that twelve years of the writer's early life were spent in active employment as a land-surveyor and valuer, during which time he lived chiefly among farmers and country people in various parts of England and Wales. The interest in agriculture and rural life then acquired has been supplemented by observation and study during recent years; and in now coming forward as a writer on the land question he is not—as is generally assumed by his critics—taking up a new and unfamiliar subject, but is returning, with wider experience and more matured judgment, to one which occupied much · of his attention during the best years of his early life.

GODALMING, *October 21st*, 1885.

CONTENTS.

PART I.

CONDITIONS AND CAUSES OF TRADE DEPRESSION.

CHAPTER I.

STATEMENT OF THE PROBLEM.

CHAPTER II.

POPULAR EXPLANATIONS OF THE DEPRESSION.

CHAPTER III.

THE CRITERIA OF A TRUE EXPLANATION.

PART II.
R E M E D I E S.

CHAPTER XIII.
FINANCIAL AND COMMERCIAL REMEDIES.

CHAPTER XIV.
THE REMEDY FOR AGRICULTURAL DEPRESSION.

CHAPTER XV.
THE REMEDY FOR RURAL DEPOPULATION.

CHAPTER XVI.
SUMMARY AND CONCLUSION.

DIAGRAMS.

:

BAD TIMES.

BAD TIMES.

PART I.

CONDITIONS AND CAUSES OF TRADE DEPRESSION.

CHAPTER I.

STATEMENT OF THE PROBLEM.

THE present Depression of Trade is remarkable, not so much for its intensity or for its extent—in both of which respects it has been equalled or surpassed on previous occasions, but for its persistence during the long period of eleven years. The late Professor Fawcett, in his *Free Trade and Protection* (p. 151), says: "The industrial depression is generally thought to have commenced in the closing months of 1874;" and during every succeeding year it has continued to be felt with more or less severity, and its remarkable persistence has been commented on by politicians and public writers. Usually a period of depression is quickly followed by one of

B

comparative prosperity. Such a reaction has been again and again predicted in this case; but up to the present time there are no satisfactory indications that the evil days are passing away. It is evident, therefore, that we are suffering in an altogether exceptional manner, that the disease of the social organism is due to causes or combinations of causes which have not been in action on former occasions, and that the remedial agencies which have been effective on former occasions of depression have now failed us.

We thus find ourselves confronted with a problem of vital importance to our well-being as a nation. We are called upon to explain why it is that, notwithstanding the exceptional advantages we possess, in an ever-increasing command over the more recondite powers of nature, an ever-increasing use of labour-saving machinery, a body of labourers whose industry and skill are proverbial, and far more complete and perfect communication with the whole world than was possessed by any previous generation —notwithstanding all these favourable conditions, which would seem to render prosperity certain, we yet find trade crippled and labour paralysed, goods of all kinds selling at unremunerative prices, yet the masses too poor to buy, and universal complaints of diminished profits and restricted markets. So long as these questions are not fully and completely answered, so long as a remedy is not found for the widespread and persistent evil which afflicts the mass of our people, our whole system of social economy, even our civilisation itself, must be accounted to be failures. It will undoubtedly be admitted that a system of society under which willing hands cannot find profitable work, and countless shops and warehouses overflowing with every necessary, comfort, and luxury, mock the longing eyes of insufficiently-clad and half-starved millions, is neither a sound nor a safe one.

We may therefore expect to find that the problem of trade-depression is fundamentally the same as that of the persistence of widespread poverty and pauperism notwithstanding our rapid and continuous growth in wealth; and if this be so, its solution will assuredly furnish us with some important principles to direct the course of future legislation. The main points of a sound political programme may be one of the important results of a successful investigation into the causes which have brought about the present depression of trade.

CHAPTER II.

NOTHING more clearly shows the necessity for a thorough and systematic inquiry into this important subject than the extraordinary diversity of opinion concerning it. Within the last few months no less than eight distinct and often opposing dicta have been put authoritatively before the public as to the extent of the depression or as to its causes. The most popular alleged cause is over-production, and this, after having been repeatedly asserted by public writers, has now been formally adopted by a resolution of the recent Trades Union Congress as being, in the opinion of the workmen of England, the most prominent cause. Many influential writers and speakers believe that our unique system of Free Trade is the chief cause of the depression, because it exposes us to an unequal competition with the products of protected countries. Others maintain the very opposite, and point out that these latter countries have suffered more depression than we have, due to their numerous and heavy protective duties checking consumption, and thus paralysing trade. The number of bad harvests that have occurred of late years is considered by some politicians to afford a sufficient explanation of the whole depression ; but, on the other hand, a writer under the authority of the Cobden Club alleges the good harvest of last year as the cause of the recent increased severity of the depression, owing to so much less shipping being required to import foreign corn, while so much less manufactured goods are needed to pay for it. Another class of writers consider that disturbances of the currency are the real cause, and that the depreciation of silver, together with the increasing scarcity of gold, will account for the whole phenomenon. Some influential authorities in the political and financial world have thrown doubt on the very existence of the depression, because, as they allege, our trade on the whole has not diminished, and therefore cannot be much depressed. Other equally good authorities admit the fact of the depression in all its extent and severity, but hold that its causes are as yet inscrutable. The late Home Secretary stated in Parliament that "No economist could satisfactorily account for the wave of depression," while the Chancellor of the Exchequer agreed with the statement, and urged it as a sufficient reason for appointing a Royal Commission to investigate the matter. We have here an amount of diversity of opinion such as exists with regard to hardly any other political or social question, and it will therefore be advisable, before proceeding to

elucidate what we conceive to be the real causes of
the depression, to state very briefly the objections to
all the suggested explanations.

In the course of the present inquiry it will become
sufficiently apparent that none of these alleged causes
separately, nor the whole of them combined, are
adequate to account for the admitted facts, one of the
most striking of these facts being that the depression
has affected, almost simultaneously, the chief great
manufacturing countries of the world. This at once
disposes of such a cause as our bad harvests, which
have been usually coincident with good harvests in
America, Australia, or other food-producing countries.
No doubt our loss by the more or less unpropitious
seasons which have prevailed for eight out of the
last twelve years has been considerable, and by
leading to the ruin of many farmers has intensified
the general depression; but this is quite a different
thing from having been a chief or primary cause
of it.

The protective tariffs of so many foreign countries
afford a more plausible cause of our depression, but
even these fail to fulfil one of the essential conditions
of a true cause. It must be remembered that the
depression began suddenly in 1874 after a long period
of great commercial prosperity. But protective
duties were not then imposed in foreign countries
for the first time, nor has it been alleged that they
were then simultaneously increased to any important
extent, while some modifications decidedly favourable
to us were made about that time. Again, there is no

country to which our exports have increased more largely since 1874 than to the United States, and it is there that protective duties are heaviest and most numerous. It is usually said that this is because we have to pay in goods for the large quantities of corn we import from America; but this is no explanation, because those who consume our goods are not those only who sell us corn, and unless we could compete with American manufacturers at their own doors, notwithstanding their protective duties, none of our goods would ever be sold there. It has, moreover, been shown by Mr. Mongredien that our exports have only diminished to certain special groups of countries, while to all other parts of the world they have either increased or have been stationary.[1] This proves that in most markets we hold our own in spite of foreign competition. It must also be remembered that our imports have continued to increase with tolerable steadiness, and on the average about in proportion to our increasing population, showing that this portion of our trade continues to flourish, but that we pay for these imports in a different way from formerly. What that way is, and how it has affected the prosperity of our trade in general, we shall see presently.

The same preliminary objection will apply to the currency theory, because both the depreciation of silver and the appreciation of gold have been very gradual processes, and it is impossible to tell when they first began to be felt in the commercial world.

[1] *Free Trade and English Commerce*, p. 65.

They can hardly, therefore, be held to account satisfactorily for a depression of trade which commenced suddenly and with great severity in a given year. The latest writer on the subject states that the decline in the output of gold began in 1865, but that the scarcity was only felt in 1880 because it took several years to absorb the previous abundance.[1] But the rapid decrease of our exports began in 1874, and 1880 was the year in which they began to increase again, so that there is really nothing but conjecture to connect the slight decrease in the gold supply with the depression. The increase in the production of silver began earlier and has been far greater than the decrease of gold. According to Del Mar, from 1848 to 1868 the world's produce of silver was between a fourth and a third in value of that of gold, while the two are now nearly equal.[2] The fact that such a great change in the proportionate produce of these two metals (added to the effect produced by two great countries—Germany and the United States — having adopted a gold instead of a silver standard for their currency) has altered the proportionate value of the latter to such a comparatively slight degree, is an indication of the enormous absorbing power of commerce and the arts for the precious metals. The value of silver only began to fall since 1871, when the price was $60\frac{7}{8}d.$ an ounce, quite up to the average price for

---

[1] "Gold Scarcity and the Depression of Trade," by Moreton Frewen. *Nineteenth Century*, October, 1875.

[2] Quoted in Kolb's *Condition of Nations*, p. 903.

many previous years, while between that date and 1882 it had steadily decreased to $51\frac{1}{2}d$. The fact that it did not fall earlier, and that the total fall is now only 15 per cent, although the quantity produced annually is double what it was fifteen years back, and the proportionate produce to that of gold so enormously increased, must cause us to doubt whether the comparatively slight diminution in the large output of gold can have had any appreciable effect in increasing its value. The large quantity of silver released by the change of the German currency in 1872 was rapidly absorbed, as shown by the greatly increased exports of bullion to India, Spain, and Portugal, during the succeeding five years.

But there is also a general argument, and I think a conclusive one, against the currency theory as affording an explanation of the depression. Mill (as well as other writers) has shown that changes in the currency, or in the absolute or relative values of gold and silver, can only affect international exchanges or uniformly raise or lower prices, but can have no effect on either wages or profits; and he further shows that whatever economical disturbance may be produced by such changes, they will only be temporary, owing to the rapidity with which re-adjustments of value and of prices are necessarily brought about. It follows that, although the depreciation of silver or the appreciation of gold may temporarily injure or benefit financiers and speculators, or those who have nominally fixed incomes payable in currency, yet it cannot alter the relative prices of labour and commodities, or so impoverish whole communities as to diminish their power of obtaining the necessaries of life. If the purchasing power of money slowly changes, this cannot permanently check either production or consumption, because both labour and goods will be equally affected by it. The well-being of the masses of every country depends primarily on their productive industry; in the second place, on their being allowed freely to exchange the products of their labour, both at home and abroad; and thirdly, on their not being impoverished by wars, or by any form of excessive taxation. None of these factors are seriously affected by slow changes in the values of the metals used for facilitating exchange. The wealth created by labour constitutes the real wealth of the world, not the tokens, whether metallic or paper, which are used to facilitate the exchange of that wealth. The true causes of universal depression must be sought in factors which either diminish productive labour or rob it of its fruits, or cause the labour of large masses of men to be directed to wasteful or injurious purposes; and it is difficult to see how a slow alteration in the relative value of the instruments of barter—an alteration which is eminently self-adjusting—can have so paralysed industry, and so impoverished the masses of consumers, as to have produced a general inability to purchase our goods over almost the whole civilised world.

Lastly, we have the doctrine of over-production;

but this is clearly a symptom, not a cause of the depression. The apparent over-production is due to a diminution of purchasing power among the masses of the people at home and abroad. Everywhere there is comparative poverty; there is abundant desire for goods, but insufficient means of satisfying the desire, and to check production will not have any tendency to increase the purchasing power of the people at large, but will assuredly diminish it. It is agreed by all political economists that general over-production is an impossibility so long as any wants remain unsatisfied. There may, it is true, be partial and local over-production, but this is quickly corrected by the self-interest of the manufacturer, and can never continue long enough to produce a lasting depression of trade.

It is not, however, denied that each of the alleged causes may produce temporary or local distress, and depression in particular industries; and this is especially the case when great fiscal changes are made in countries with which we trade largely; and above all, when, by means of bounties on exportation, goods, on the manufacture of which a large amount of capital and labour is engaged, are able to be sold here at less than the real cost of manufacture and delivery. In these cases the corresponding industries in this country are injured and sometimes ruined, capital has to seek other employment, the buildings and plant used in the manufacture are often rendered worthless, and numbers of workmen are thrown out of employment, and, having special

skill in this one industry only, often suffer great distress before they can obtain fresh employment. The depression and suffering thus caused in some trades is very great, and is not sufficiently recognised; but this is quite a different thing from a general depression affecting all the staple industries of the country at once, and extending even to those countries which are usually supposed to benefit at our expense.

The question is far too wide, the problem too general, to be solved by a reference to individual cases of hardship; and it is much to be feared that the Royal Commission now sitting will result in bringing together a vast and often conflicting mass of facts and opinions in reference to particular industries to the entire neglect of those more general facts and conditions which can alone furnish the true solution.

Having thus briefly indicated the reasons why the causes hitherto alleged are inadequate, we will now proceed to consider what are the main features of the depression, and what are the essential criteria by which its real causes may be distinguished.

CHAPTER III.

DEPRESSION of trade may be succinctly defined as a widespread diminution in the demand for our chief manufactures, both at home and abroad. Our productive power seems to exceed the purchasing power of our own country and of the world at large. Our customers have either become poorer or they buy in other markets. The consequence is that manufactories and workshops work short time or are closed, wages are lowered, strikes take place to resist the lowering of wages, shopkeepers do a diminished trade, the traffic receipts of railroads fall off or increase but slowly, and there is, almost universally, a complaint that times are hard and trade is bad. Hence competition increases in severity, the prices of goods fall, and numerous failures and bankruptcies are the result. In the present case we find, that from 1870 to 1875 the total number of bankruptcies and compositions with creditors rose gradually from 5,002 to 7,899; but in the next four years, when the depression had fully set in, they increased rapidly,

year by year, till they reached 13,132 in 1879.
Since that date they have somewhat decreased, but
were still over 9,000 in 1882 and 8,555 in 1883.
The low prices of goods, the number of men out of
employment, and the numerous bankruptcies, afford
statistical evidence of the depression in our home
trade.

As regards our foreign trade, equally clear evidence
is afforded by a consideration of the progress of our
exports during the last twenty years. From 1864
to 1873 these rose continuously and rapidly, and we
had then a time of unexampled commercial prosperity. In 1874 they began to decline, and this
decline continued for six consecutive years, when
the decrease had reached the amount of sixty-five
millions. In 1880 they began to rise again, but
even in 1883 had not reached the level of the years
1872 and 1873. Such a great and continuous
decrease in our export trade has not occurred during
the last half century. (See Diagram, p. 19.)

All this time, as has been already stated, our
imports continued to increase, subject only to minor
fluctuations. Up to 1873 the increase was rapid;
from that date more slow and irregular. but on the
whole in full proportion to the increase of our
population. It thus appears that, while we have
continued to purchase largely of foreign countries,
these countries, or some of them, have ceased to
purchase our goods in like proportion. It is also
generally admitted that the depression has affected
simultaneously all the great manufacturing countries

of the world, and that in these also there has been a falling off of customers; whence we arrive at the startling but inevitable conclusion that the total demand for the staple manufactures of the world has diminished in proportion to population, and, as we cannot suppose the needs or the desires of mankind have diminished, it must be that they have become less able to purchase, in other words that they have become poorer.

It is, therefore, clear that, in order to show that any alleged cause of the depression is a true cause, it must be proved that, either directly or indirectly, it impoverishes or otherwise diminishes the purchasing power of some considerable body of our customers; and further, that it is a cause which either began to act at, or shortly before, the first appearance of the depression, or became greatly intensified in its action about that time; and yet again, that it has continued in action for several years, or is still acting. We must therefore exclude such causes as drunkenness and the drink traffic generally, because, although they undoubtedly impoverish large bodies of our customers and render them less able to purchase other manufactured goods, yet, as there is no proof that these causes have increased during the last ten or fifteen years, but rather the contrary, they cannot be correctly alleged as being among the actual producing causes of the present evil. Yet the diminution of drunkenness would undoubtedly alleviate the depression, and, so great is the amount spent in alcoholic drinks—about one hundred and thirty-six millions annually, or more than double the rental of all the farms in the United Kingdom —that there is ample room for an improvement which would set free a vast income for general expenditure and greatly revivify trade. But it may be doubted whether relief thus gained would be permanent, because, the efficient causes which have actually brought about the present depression continuing in action they would again impoverish our customers, and the evil days would certainly come back to us.

There are, however, several causes which fully comply with the conditions here laid down as characterising a *vera causa* of trade depression, and which are also, in their combined action, fully adequate to account for the existing depression in all its wide extent and almost unexampled persistence. I now propose to consider these in some detail, taking them, to the best of my judgment, in the order of their relative importance.

CHAPTER IV.

FOREIGN LOANS.

THE most flourishing period of the British commerce was from 1870 to 1875, the culminating years being 1872 and 1873. It was to this latter period that Mr. Gladstone applied his celebrated expression of our commercial prosperity advancing " by leaps and bounds," apparently without any conception of the unsound basis on which this sudden burst of prosperity rested, or any prevision of the reckoning that was soon to follow.

The special feature of our commerce to which we now have to direct attention is the remarkable change that has taken place in the relative amount of our exports and imports. During the whole of our prosperous epoch as well as afterwards, and even down to the present time, our imports have continued to increase at a moderate rate, though somewhat more rapidly since 1879, in consequence of the bad harvests necessitating larger imports of food. Our exports, on the other hand, increased with enormous rapidity, reached a maximum in 1872-3, and then as rapidly declined. (See Diagram I.). The excess of our exports during the years 1870-75 over those of the

C

preceding and succeeding quinquennial periods was
nearly 250 millions sterling. How was this enormous
increase of our exports paid for ?   Certainly not by
imported goods, for these had increased at a far less
rapid rate.   But the records of the money-market
supply the answer.   During the years 1870-75 there
was almost a mania for foreign government loans,
which we supplied to the amount of about 260
millions, [1] besides other large sums subscribed to
railways and numerous other undertakings in all
parts of the world.

It is a well-known fact that these great loans are
never advanced by the lenders in the form of actual
money, but by bills of exchange or by credits on
foreign banks, and further, that the accounts between
the two countries are ultimately balanced as far as
possible by means of merchandise transmitted from
the lending country.   It is thus often said, though
not quite accurately, that the loans are advanced in
goods and not in money.   What actually occurs seems
to be that the money (bills or credit) received by the
borrowing government is, in part, and often wholly
spent at once in public works, in salaries, or in other
modes of less productive expenditure, in any case
leading to enormous imports of goods, such as railway-
iron, engines or machinery, or of such cotton or other
fabrics as are most used in the country, or of furniture,
ornaments, or jewellery, the demand for all or any of
which may be largely increased by the flood of money

---

[1] These figures have been obtained from the lists of foreign loans
in Abbott's *Stock and Share Almanack.*

DIAGRAM I.

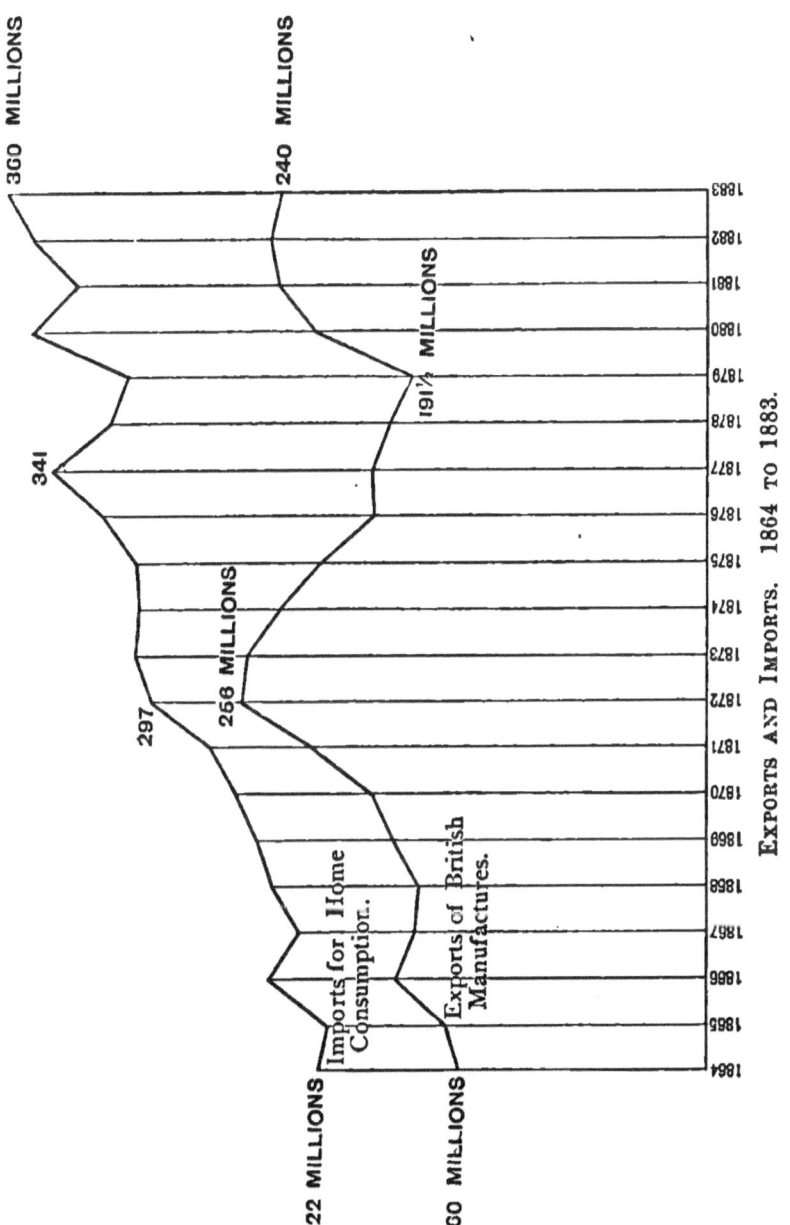

EXPORTS AND IMPORTS. 1864 TO 1883.

360 MILLIONS

240 MILLIONS

191½ MILLIONS

341

297

266 MILLIONS

Imports for Home Consumption.

Exports of British Manufactures.

222 MILLIONS

160 MILLIONS

1864 1865 1866 1867 1868 1869 1870 1871 1872 1873 1874 1875 1876 1877 1878 1879 1880 1881 1882 1883

c 2

being rapidly squandered. In this way a great demand arose for our manufactures; and as our loans extended all over the world, embracing besides Egypt, Turkey, Russia, Austria, Italy, and Spain in Europe ; Brazil, Peru, Chile and Paraguay in South America; Costa Rica, Mexico, Guatemala, Honduras, and the United States in North America ; Japan in the East, and almost the whole of our Colonies, the entire range of our manufactures in turn felt the influence, and an era of high-pressure prosperity set in. The natural result was the undue extension of many manufactures by capitalists competing for the golden harvest. New mills or factories with the most perfect machinery were erected, and others were extended or improved so as to turn out the greatest quantity of finished goods in the smallest possible time. But soon came the inevitable reaction. The vast amounts of borrowed capital were exhausted, and instead of having a plethora of money to spend all these countries had interest to pay, and the people being heavily taxed to pay this interest their purchasing power was diminished, and the demand for our goods suddenly fell off. Henceforth, therefore, while the imports needed to supply our own necessities went on increasing with our increasing population, our exports decreased. This decrease necessarily caused much depression and distress, and it had an element of permanence, because so large a part of the money had been expended *unproductively*, adding nothing to the real wealth of the borrowing countries, while the debt remained to bear interest and sometimes to be paid

off by means of a sinking fund. Still, some of the
countries we lent money to did expend it on useful
works, and where population was increasing and
government was not altogether bad there would be
some increased demand for our goods, so that in the
course of a few years we might have expected some
improvement. But other pernicious causes were at
work during the very same period which tended to
increase and perpetuate the mischief.

During the years 1867-75 there was a great rail-
way-making mania in the United States; more than
forty thousand miles of new lines were constructed
in nine years, and no less than 7,112 miles were
made in 1872. A large part of the iron used in the
construction of these lines was bought in England,
causing a great demand for iron and coal. The
profits from these minerals became enormous,
capitalists rushed to invest in them, and new mines
were opened or old ones reworked at great cost and
to an extent far beyond the permanent demand.
We all remember the coal famine of 1873, which
marked the culminating point of the speculative
fever, and which is said to have put sixty-six
millions of money into the pockets of the mine
owners.[1] The Franco-German and Russo-Turkish
wars still further contributed to inflate our industries
by the demand for war material and general supplies,
and, as a consequence, shipbuilding was greatly extended, and was persevered in till we now possess a

---

[1] *Free Trade and Protection*, by the Right Hon. H. Fawcett, M.P.,
p. 153. Fifth Edition.

far larger amount of shipping than we can profitably employ. The result has been widespread loss and suffering—unremunerative freights in consequence of the competition of shipowners seeking employment for their vessels, silent building yards, and distressed workmen.[1]

I have thus endeavoured to show what are the effects of our enormous foreign loans, and how they have assisted in bringing about the depression under which we are suffering; but the question is such a very important one, and its true bearings are so often misunderstood that a little further elucidation seems necessary. It is usually stated, without qualification, that we do not pay money for our imports or receive money for our exports, but that we really exchange them; and Mr. Mongredien, in his *Free Trade and English Commerce*, thus explains the bearing of this doctrine on the point we are discussing. He says:—
" Some nations export more than they import because they are in debt to the rest of the world. These debts are provided for, not by the transmission of specie, but by the export of goods, and for that portion of their exports these countries, of course, receive no imports in return. So likewise some countries (among which England stands foremost) import more than they export, because the rest of the world is in debt to them, and this excess of imports being sent in payment of that debt no return is made for it in the shape of exports." He further

---

[1] See an article by S. Williamson, M.P. (himself a shipowner), in the *Fortnightly Review*, January, 1885.

proves that this is what really occurs, by showing, that during the very time that we are receiving a large surplus of imports there is no corresponding flow of gold from the country to pay for them; and also, that the amount of these surplus imports corresponds pretty nearly with the amount of interest on foreign loans, &c., held in this country.[1]

These statements, though truly representing the general results, do not accurately or sufficiently explain them. A loan to a foreign state is not *necessarily* advanced in goods, or even balanced by an export of goods from the lending country. Whether it is so or not will entirely depend on how the money is spent. The millions subscribed by France, and paid for forced labour in constructing the Suez Canal, did not imply a corresponding export of goods from France or from any other country, because the labourers were paid barely sufficient for subsistence, while their farms deteriorated in their absence, and they were thus even less able to purchase foreign manufactures than before. So, on the other hand, the payment of interest by borrowing states would not *necessarily* diminish either their desire for our goods or their power of purchasing them, *if the loans had been all wisely and productively employed*, for in that case the whole country would have been benefited, and the people would have been quite as well able to purchase from us as before. A loan judiciously expended makes the borrower richer than

---

[1] *Free Trade and English Commerce*, p. 88. Also Fawcett's *Free Trade and Protection*, p. 149.

before, even after he has repaid it, while one inju-
diciously expended leaves him poorer, even while the
debt remains unpaid ; and this is true of nations as
well as of individuals. It follows, that the real
reason of the decrease of our exports to the countries
which have contracted large loans (and Mr. Mongredien shows [1] that it is to these countries alone
that our exports have largely diminished) is, that the
money has been used *unproductively*, being expended
in wars and war-materials, or in useless public works,
or squandered in supporting the luxury or gratifying
the whims and passions of despotic rulers. The
people, therefore, on whose custom the welfare of
our manufactures chiefly depends, are no better off,
and often even worse off, than before ; while the
heavy load of taxation required to pay interest and
sinking fund, not merely on the money received but
also on the large portion absorbed by financiers and
agents, greatly diminishes their power of purchasing
foreign goods. Hence it follows, as might have been
anticipated, that it is the *purpose* for which the loan
is required, or to which it is applied, that determines
whether its effects shall be good or evil ; and it is
because the greater part of the foreign loans of
recent times have been essentially *immoral*, inasmuch as they have been made in order to support
war and conquest, or to pander to the vices or the
speculations of despotic rulers, that they have caused
nothing but evil to all concerned, laying a heavy
burden of taxation on the people of the borrowing

[1] *Free Trade and English Commerce*, p. 65.

State, thereby checking trade in the lending
State, and producing general distress among her
workers.

Mr. Mongredien maintains, however, that the
excess of imports over exports (or more properly the
diminution of our exports in proportion to our imports) is " a sign not of our decay but of our wealth,"
and he rejoices over it accordingly.[1] This may be
the case as regards our *aggregate* nominal wealth,
but, if so, it affords a good illustration of the important truth that riches are no indication of national
well-being. The wealth which has thus increased is
chiefly that of great financiers, speculators, and merchants, and the excessive accumulations of these
millionaires tends directly, as will be shown further
on, to increase and perpetuate the general depression
of trade.

Before quitting this important part of our subject
I will endeavour by a familiar illustration to render
more clear and intelligible the injurious effects on
trade of large and indiscriminate loans. Let us
suppose the case of a prosperous country town
where all the traders and mechanics are doing a
steady business. Some money-lenders now appear,
ready to advance money to all who want it, and on
the most speculative securities; and so all the idle
and spendthrifts, the expectant heirs, or those who
have reversions to property, as well as many of the
more sanguine of the farmers, mechanics, and

---

[1] Prof. Fawcett held the same opinion; see *Free Trade and
Protection*, p. 148.

labourers, get as much money as they want at high rates of interest. This goes on for a few years, and of course, the spending of all this money causes a great apparent increase of prosperity in the town. Tradesmen, merchants, and mechanics, all find their business increase, and thinking the good times will last, they enlarge their premises, increase their stocks of goods, and take on fresh workmen. But at length most of the money is spent, and the money-lenders stop further supplies, and then there inevitably sets in a period of slackness and depression proportional to the previous prosperity. Those who had spent their borrowed money unproductively are now worse off than ever, having to pay heavy interest and instalments of the capital. Expenditure everywhere has to be reduced; many become poor and some are ruined; and the tradesmen and merchants suddenly find their shops and warehouses empty of customers, and complain loudly of the inexplicable depression of trade.

But the effect of the indiscriminate foreign loans of our capitalists and financiers is exactly the same on a larger scale, because our trade extends over the whole world, and our very best customers—the masses of the people in each country—are taxed and impoverished in order to pay the usurious interest on these loans, and are therefore not able to consume their accustomed supply of our manufactures.

CHAPTER V.

SINCE the year 1870, but more especially since 1874, the general war expenditure of Europe has increased enormously. This is partly a consequence of the Franco-German war which so greatly enhanced the military power of United Germany and led other nations to aim at a corresponding increase in their forces, and in part to the enormously increased cost of iron-clad ships, monster guns, torpedoes, and all the scientific appliances of modern warfare.

Up to the year 1875 our own army and navy had increased but little for many years, the total expenditure in 1874 being £24,664,000, which was somewhat less than that of 1864. But since the former date our outlay on the two services has risen greatly and now amounts to £28,964,000, an increase of more than four millions. The number of men has increased from 189,000 in 1874 to 197,000 in 1884, exclusive of the Indian army.

In most of the great states of Europe the increase

both of men and of war expenditure has been far greater than ours. Austria up to 1874 spent less than seven millions on her army: she now spends £13,433,000, with an increase of about fifteen thousand men. France has increased her forces by fifty thousand men in the last ten years; while her military and naval expenditure has nearly doubled since the war, and now reaches the enormous sum of £35,500,000. Germany during the same period has raised her war expenditure by more than three millions, the present amount being £20,050,000. Italy has doubled her war expenses since 1873. In that year they were a little over nine millions, now they are £18,900,000. Russia has followed the same course, having increased her war expenditure from less than twenty millions in 1870 to £33,000,000 in 1884.

The loss involved in these huge armaments is of three distinct kinds. First, by the number of men, mostly in the prime of life and of the very best physique, who are kept idle or unproductively employed; secondly, by the burden of increased taxation which the rest of the community have to bear; and thirdly, by the actual destruction of life and property in war, which, wherever it occurs, inevitably diminishes for a time the productive and purchasing powers of that country. Let us endeavour to form some conception of the amount of loss due to each of these causes.

From information given in successive issues of the *Statesman's Year Book*, it appears that, since 1870, the armies and navies of Europe have been increased by about 630,000 men on the peace establishments. This number of men, therefore, has been wholly withdrawn from productive labour; but during periods of war a much larger number is thus withdrawn, and the country is, to that extent, still further impoverished. But the total number thus withdrawn, though very large—the standing armies and navies of Europe being estimated at 3,683,706 men—represents only a portion, and perhaps even a small portion, of the mischief done, since the numbers employed in the equipment of this force, and in the production of the vast and complex war-material now used are, not improbably, very much greater, and these are all equally lost for productive purposes. If we think of the hundreds of huge iron-clad ships which have recently been built, and try to form a conception of the number of men employed upon them directly and indirectly—from those who dug out the iron ore, and the coal used to smelt the ore, to those who construct the huge and beautifully finished marine engines—from the men who felled the trees in Canadian and Indian forests to the skilled workmen who design and frame and finish with elaborate care the whole of the internal fittings—we shall be convinced that to build one of these monster vessels requires from first to last a small army of men, all of whose labour, so far as any benefit to mankind is concerned, might as well have been employed in pumping water out of the sea and allowing it to flow back again. Then consider the equipment, clothes, arms, and ammunition of all these great European armies ; the manufactories of powder and explosives, the monster guns and projectiles, the rockets and torpedoes, the horses and horse accoutrements, and all the innumerable variety of stores that are required to supply a modern army in the field — and then follow back every one of these things to the raw material brought from various parts of the world, and to the numerous processes of manufacture through which it has to pass — and further consider the amount of purely intellectual power required, the origination and improvement and detailed designs for the rifles and cannons, the projectiles and explosives, the pontoons, the fortifications, the torpedo-boats, and the iron-clads—and we shall probably think it not an extravagant estimate that for every ten thousand men in a modern army and navy at least another ten thousand are wholly employed in making the necessary equipment and war material, the labour of the whole twenty thousand being utterly wasted, inasmuch as all that they produce is consumed, not merely unproductively and uselessly, but destructively. We may fairly estimate, then, that the military preparedness of modern Europe involves a total loss to the community of the labour of about SEVEN MILLIONS of men, and a corresponding amount of animal and mechanical power and of labour-saving machinery. If, now, we consider that the weight of guns, the thickness of armour-plating, the size and engine-power of ships, and the complex requirements of an army in the field, have all been rapidly increasing during the last ten or fifteen years, we may fairly estimate that one-fourth or one-fifth of this number of men have been abstracted from the productive workers of Europe during the last ten years, the period over which the commercial depression has extended.

Let us next consider the heavy burden of taxation upon all the chief European peoples, the increase of which during recent years has been almost wholly caused by increased military expenditure and the interest on debts incurred for wars or preparations for war, for fortifications or for military railways. This increase may be best estimated by comparing the expenditure of 1870, the year before the Franco-German war, with that of 1884. During this period of fourteen years our own expenditure has increased from £75,000,000 to £87,000,000; that of Austria from £55,000,000 to £94,000,000; that of France from £85,000,000 to £142 500,000; that of Germany from £54,000,000 to £112,500,000; that of Italy from £40,000,000 to £61,500,000; and that of Russia from £66,000,000 to £114,500,000. Altogether the expenditure of the six great powers of Europe has increased from £345,000,000 to £612,000,000, an additional burthen of £266,500,000 a year. The population of these six states is now a little over 269 millions, so that they have to bear, on the average, an addition of taxation amounting to nearly a pound a head, or about five pounds for each family, a most oppressive amount when we consider the extreme poverty of the masses in all these states, and that even before this period of inflated war-expenditure they had already to support a heavy and often an almost unbearable load of taxation. We must therefore admit that this great addition to their fiscal burdens in the last fourteen years must have seriously diminished the purchasing power of more than two hundred millions of people, and this alone is calculated to produce, and must actually produce, a depression of trade in all the countries which supply their wants, and therefore in none more seriously than in our own.

There remains yet to be considered the injury done by the actual destruction of life and property which occurs whenever this elaborate and costly war-machinery is put to its destined use. Owing to the wide extent and endless ramifications of modern commerce wherever life and property are destroyed by war all nations with an extensive foreign trade must feel some of the consequences. When villages and towns are burnt or bombarded, crops devastated and domestic animals taken by invading armies, troops quartered on the inhabitants and forced contributions made, the result must be the impoverishment of the population for several years. For a long time they have a severe struggle even to exist. Their houses have to be rebuilt, their lands to be again cultivated, seed and domestic animals to be procured, fresh capital to be accumulated; and till all this is done they have no means of purchasing foreign goods or of indulging in anything beyond the barest necessaries of life. And when the war is long

D

and destructive there is, in addition, the loss of
human life, not merely by slaughter in battle, but
by the distress and exposure, the disease and famine
which are the inevitable consequences of war, a loss
often to be counted, not merely by thousands and
tens of thousands but even by millions. And all
these lost lives are, from our present point of view,
lost customers, and thus still further increase the sum
total of injury to commerce which war produces.

Now, during the last twenty years there have been
a continued series of wars which have all, more or
less, tended to produce these injurious effects. Beginning with the New Zealand war in 1865, we
have in succession the Abyssinian war of 1867, the
great Franco-German war of 1871-72, the Ashantee
war in 1875, the terrible Russo-Turkish war of
1878, the Transvaal, Zulu, and other South African
wars of 1879-80, the Afghan war of 1881, the
Egyptian war of 1883, and the Soudan war perhaps
not yet concluded. Who can calculate the amount
of life and property destroyed, and the consequent
misery and impoverishment of large populations
during these twenty years? Traders have, unfortun-
ately, often considered war to be advantageous to
them, on account of the rapid and reckless expenditure of public money on war materials and stores,
and the opportunity of making large profits by war
contracts. But this is a very partial effect and
limited to but few departments of trade, while the
depressing effect of war, in the increased taxation
it always involves and in the impoverishment of

our customers which it always produces, is certain, widespread, and often enduring. The recent wars in Egypt and the Soudan, whatever other results they may have, will assuredly have the effect of tending still further to prolong and intensify our commercial depression.

If our manufacturers and merchants as a body would consider this question in all its bearings they would surely arrive at the conclusion that all war wherever or by whomsoever waged, is bad for trade, since it impoverishes alike the winner and the loser the invader and the invaded, while it inevitably destroys a number of actual or possible customers. The moral arguments against war would doubtless be more generally effective if it were clearly seen that, always and everywhere, its direct and necessary effect is to produce more or less of depression of trade.

But if war injures the capitalist, the manufacturer, and the trader, still more does it injure the worker, and on this point I cannot do better than quote the forcible words of Mr. Mongredien.[1] After describing the various destructive agencies and methods of war, he says: "As wealth dwindles somebody must suffer, and the suffering mainly falls on the poor and weak. The capitalist is mulcted of part of his wealth, but he can wait. The labour-seller is mulcted of the necessaries of life, and he and his dear ones cannot wait. The less there is to produce the less there is to distribute. Need we say which class it

---

[1] *Wealth Creation*, by Augustus Mongredien, p. 115.

is that will run short ?   It is on you, labour-sellers
of the world, that the burden chiefly falls.   It is you
who are the slayers and the slain.   You form the
rank and file who deal the blows and on whom the
blows are dealt.   To your chiefs belong the honour
and the rewards.   As for you, you are under contract
to suffer and to cause suffering ; to inflict and to
endure death ; to destroy instead of creating wealth ;
and to use every effort to suppress the fund out of
which labour is paid.   The war-system, pernicious
to every class, is a special curse to yours.   Are you
content to view it as a necessity ?   In this our pro-
test against it, we look for your special assistance by
thought, word, and pen.   Public opinion is made up
of assenting units."   Since these words were written
the working-men of England have obtained the
means not only of verbally protesting, but of actually
deciding against war, if it so pleases them.   If they
will vote for no representatives but such as will
pledge themselves to oppose all but strictly defen-
sive wars, and never to begin a war until we are
actually attacked, then war will rarely occur, war
expenditure will be reduced, and, so soon as other
nations follow our example and that of the United
States, one of the chief causes of depression of
trade will cease to exist.

CHAPTER VI.

RURAL DEPOPULATION.

DURING the first half of the present century every county in England and Wales continued to increase in population at each successive census, until, in 1861, *three* agricultural counties—Cambridgeshire, Norfolk, and Huntingdonshire—showed a slight decrease. In 1871 *eight* counties showed a diminished population, some of them to a considerable amount; while in 1881 the decrease had extended to *fourteen* counties, and in *ten* others there was a very small increase. In these latter counties it is found that one or two towns have usually increased more than the whole county, so that here also the rural districts must have suffered a considerable diminution of population. But these statements by no means give an adequate expression of the facts, for a closer examination of the Census Returns shows us that the diminution of the population of rural England has not been confined to any limited portion of it, but really extends, with very few exceptions, over the whole country; though, when counties or large divisions of counties, are compared, the real facts are obscured by the increase of the numerous towns.

The Preliminary Report of the last census gives, in Table XI., the population of all the Registration Sub-Districts in England and Wales for the years 1871 and 1881, showing the increase or decrease in the ten years. There are 2,175 of these sub-districts, which are about the size of very large parishes, and the number in each county is thus sufficiently great to afford a tolerably correct notion of the area over which the diminution of population really extends. In order that the reader may be able to see at a glance the results furnished by this large body of figures, I have prepared a diagrammatic table (given opposite), which exhibits by a partially shaded band the proportionate number of sub-districts in each county in which the population has decreased, while the two columns of figures give the actual population of these sub-districts, and their numerical decrease for each county. Middlesex and London have been omitted; and when a diminution of the population of certain sub-districts in large towns has occurred these have also been omitted, as they are due to houses being removed to make way for railway-stations, new streets, public buildings, or other municipal works. The diagram, therefore, will show, pretty accurately, the extent of rural depopulation. It will be seen that this exists over the larger part of all the agri-cultural counties, except those portions which form residential districts around London; while even in the manufacturing counties considerable areas

DIAGRAMMATIC TABLE (II.)

Showing the Proportionate Number of the Registration Sub-Districts in each County of England and Wales in which the Population has diminished in the Ten Years, 1871—81. There are 2,175 Sub-Districts.

Names of Counties.	The Shaded portion of the Band gives the proportion of Sub-Districts with Decreasing Population.	Decreasing Areas. Population in 1881.	Amount of Decrease since 1871.
Surrey		30,000	300
Kent		133,000	3,318
Sussex		46,000	2,370
Hampshire		136,000	4,762
Berkshire		64,000	4,173
Hertfordshire		73,000	3,070
Buckinghamshire ...		63,000	5,990
Oxfordshire		95,000	6,893
Northamptonshire ...		89,000	4,928
Huntingdonshire ...		51,000	4,828
Bedfordshire............		83,000	5,857
Cambridgeshire		121,000	8,451
Essex		184,000	11,881
Suffolk		194,000	12,597
Norfolk...		214,000	8,890
Wiltshire		170,000	10,803
Dorsetshire		110,000	11,087
Devonshire		298,000	23,483
Cornwall		196,000	36,767
Somersetshire		263,000	17,277
Gloucestershire		129,000	9,364
Herefordshire		79,000	5,643
Shropshire		146,000	8,193
Staffordshire		148,000	7,084
Worcestershire.........		53,000	2,977
Leicestershire		46,000	2,274

DIAGRAMMATIC TABLE (II.) *continued.*

Counties.	Decreasing Sub-Districts Shaded.	Population of Decreasing Areas in 1881.	Amount of Decrease since 1871.
Warwickshire		58,000	3,156
Rutlandshire		20,000	484
Lincolnshire		174,000	11,492
Nottinghamshire		53,000	3,459
Derbyshire		21,000	1,426
Cheshire		42,000	1,435
Lancashire		31,000	1,271
Yorkshire, W.R.		125,000	7,460
,, E.R.		72,000	3,008
,, N.R.		85,000	6,337
Durham		60,000	6,156 .
Northumberland		48,000	5,085
Cumberland		41,000	3,565
Westmoreland		20,000	2,646
Monmouthshire		49,000	3,237
Glamorganshire		101,000	5,669
Carmarthenshire		53,000	1,485
Pembrokeshire		39,000	2,102
Cardiganshire		56,000	4,000
Brecknockshire		43,000	3,393 ,
Radnorshire		13,000	1,335
Montgomeryshire		60,000	3,744
Flintshire		19,000	526
Denbighshire		27,000	1,449
Merionethshire			
Carnarvonshire		18,000	217
Anglesea		25,000	1,524
Totals		4,567,000	308,941

Population of Decreasing Sub-Districts in 1871 4,876,000
Normal Increase of Rural Population at 17 per cent. 828,900
Population calculated for 1881 at normal increase 5,704,900
Actual Population in 1881 4,567,000

Real Exodus of Population from the Decreasing Sub-Districts ... 1,137,900 have suffered in the same way. The total decrease of the population of these rural areas in ten years amounted to 308,941.

This number, large as it is, represents, however, only a small portion of the migration that has gone on from country to town. The average increase of the whole population in the period referred to was about 14½ per cent., and it is well known that the normal increase of the rural is much greater than that of the urban population. The births in the country are about 3 per cent. more, the deaths about 10 per cent. less; so that we cannot put the normal increase of the purely rural population at less than about 17 per cent. But the population of the

diminishing areas in 1871 was . . .	4,876,000
Normal increase, at 17 per cent.. .	828,900
Population should have been . .	5,704,900
The actual population in 1881 is .	4,567,000
The actual reduction is therefore .	1,137,900

We thus see that the real measure of the exodus of the people from these particular areas is consider-ably more than one million. But even this by no means represents the full measure of the rural depopulation; for, besides these areas in which the population has actually decreased, there is a large additional area over which they have increased less than the normal 17 per cent., and from which there must therefore have been some migration. Taking, for example, a few typical counties, I find that in

Sussex, which shows but a small absolute decrease, the whole county, except a few towns and their suburban districts, has increased much below the normal rate, implying migration of the surplus rural population to the towns. In Hampshire the same thing occurs, only Portsmouth, Southampton, and Christchurch having increased up to or beyond the normal rate. In Buckinghamshire not a single sub-district has increased normally. In Norfolk the same. In Leicestershire only the towns and some of their suburban districts have increased normally. In Derbyshire only nine out of twenty-five sub-districts have increased up to the normal standard. In Cumberland the seaports only have increased normally, the rest of the county showing a very slight increase, or none. The conclusion we arrive at, therefore, is, that over the whole of rural England there has been a continuous flow of population to the great towns, owing to the natural increase of the people not finding the means of existence elsewhere; and if for the migration from those sub-districts which increased less than the normal rate (and large numbers of them have hardly increased at all) we add three-quarters of a million, we shall find that a total of nearly *two millions of people* have, in the short space of ten years, been forced by the struggle for existence to leave the country for the towns!

Another important fact we have to note is, that the decrease of agricultural labourers is given in the census as about 90,000 only, so that with their families they will not account for much more than one-fourth the migrating population ; and this agrees with much independent evidence that small tradesmen, shopkeepers, and mechanics have also left the rural districts for the towns. This vast migration is an indication of want and hopelessness; and the constant inpouring to the towns is universally admitted to have been one of the chief causes of that widespread and terrible distress which now pervades the metropolis and almost all our great cities.

One of the direct and immediate results of the transference of nearly two million people from country to town is to diminish our production of food. A considerable proportion of these families kept pigs and poultry, and some a cow or a few sheep, while vegetables and fruit were grown by almost all. The enormous increase in the imports of such articles of food as bacon, butter, cheese, eggs, poultry, and potatoes, during the last forty years, has been adduced by Mr. Giffen as proving the increased well-being of the working classes, but a large portion of it is certainly due to *decrease of production*, owing to the decrease of country-dwelling labourers. If we look at the importations of the following special products of the rural industrial classes, we shall see plainly the loss we have sustained by driving them into the towns:—

	Imports in 1870.	Imports in 1883.
Bacon and Pork	863,000 cwt.	5,007,000 cwt.
Potatoes	127,000 cwt.	4,034,000 cwt.
Eggs	430 millions	814 millions.

It is absurd to suppose that our consumption can have increased to this enormous extent during a period of commercial depression; but a large portion, if not the whole, of this excess of imports may be explained by the fact that these articles were formerly produced by the millions of labourers and others who have left our depopulated rural parishes, or by the farmers who employed them. It must always be remembered that a large part of the value of this food is dead loss to us, since it was and still would have been mainly produced by the utilisation of time and labour otherwise wasted. And much of it was also a clear gain to the labourer, and was chiefly spent by him in home manufactures; so that the loss of all this is a very important cause of depression of trade. Two millions of customers impoverished by a forced change of their conditions of life is a factor which cannot be neglected.

It may be objected that the land is still cultivated and produces crops of equal value to those obtained by the departed cottagers. Even if this were true it would not affect the argument, because they, our best customers, are none the less impoverished. But it is not true. There is abundant evidence to show that garden or allotment land produces many times over what is obtained from farm land. Lord Carrington recently stated that his allotments near High Wycombe produced an average of 40*l.* an acre as against 7*l.* an acre, the most which a farmer could get out of the land; and Mr. Bailey Denton, in his treatise on the agricultural labourer, estimates that a rood of ground will yield him a net profit of 4l. a year. The loss by the transference of a million of labourers and other working men from their rural homes to the great cities is thus a real and very important loss to the community.

But, again, it may be said, they are still consumers, whether they live in country or in town; and it cannot make much difference to the trade of the country where they live. This, however, is another error. When they go to London, as so many of them go, they rapidly die off. The death-rate of the rural population of England for 1881 was 16·8 per thousand, while that of East London, which is the type of such districts as the poor live in, was 24·2 per thousand. Thus, of a million of emigrants to London, in ten years 74,000 more will have died than if they had remained at home. The birth-rate also is much lower, and it has been stated on good authority that the permanently resident population of London would actually diminish were it not for the constant inflow from the country. Again, large numbers of these immigrants become pauperised, they wear only second-hand clothing, and almost entirely cease to be customers for manufactured goods, so that the loss to the staple manufactures of the country is very great. Rural depopulation must therefore be held to be a direct and very important cause of depression of trade.

CHAPTER VII.

IF the facts and inferences set forth in some detail in the last chapter are correct it necessarily follows that the masses of the people are on the whole worse off than they were ten years ago; in other words, that poverty and destitution are increasing, in extent if not in intensity. It is, however, continually asserted that pauperism is diminishing over the whole country as well as in London, and that the working classes have never been so well off. But if this is really the case there should be no diminution in the demand for manufactured goods, and depression of the home trade ought not to exist. It is therefore necessary to examine this assertion and the grounds on which it rests. Our public writers and speakers, including members of parliament and of the government, continually adduce the official Poor Law statistics as proving that pauperism has diminished; but I venture to assert that the conclusion is altogether erroneous, because officially-relieved paupers form but a part, and perhaps only a

small part, of the whole number of individuals who
depend upon extraneous relief for some portion of
their subsistence.

Official paupers are either outdoor or indoor. The
former have greatly diminished during the last ten
or fifteen years, while the latter have increased at as
great a rate as the population (see Diagram, p. 49).
But it is well known that during this period outdoor
relief has been steadily discouraged by the Poor Law
authorities, and to such an extent that it has been
almost abolished in many unions. In Whitechapel,
Stepney, and St. George's-in-the-East, outdoor paupers have diminished from many thousands to a few
hundreds or even less. In Stepney they were reduced from 7,602 to 263 in ten years, while indoor
paupers did not increase, because private charity,
extended and organised, took its place. In Whitechapel the number of outdoor paupers was 2,768 in
1870 and only 20 in 1884, and here there has
actually been an accompanying diminution of indoor
paupers, the alleged cause being that charity is so well
systematised by the Charity Organisation Society,
and by many earnest workers, that voluntary effort
has completely taken the place of outdoor relief.

An examination of the voluminous "Register"
issued by the above-named Society shows how
largely charitable societies and allied organisations
have increased of late years. Since 1860 there have
been established no less than 60 distinct Associations
for the relief of temporary distress, besides 20 new
Reformatories, Industrial Schools, Training Ships

and Children's Homes; 15 Societies for the relief of convicts and penitents; 12 for aiding servants out of work, besides 25 Associations or individuals who have provided improved dwellings for the poor. These are all general in their character and aim, but there are also an immense number of local institutions and societies in every parish and district of London, as well as all over the country. To give an idea of their number I may state that the parish of Paddington alone has 70 such societies, a considerable proportion of which are of recent origin. Now this vast increase of charitable means and benevolent exertion, aided by more intelligence and organisation, must everywhere, to a large extent, have taken the place of parish relief and rendered it unnecessary, as we see that it has actually done in the above-quoted districts of East London.

Yet in spite of all this effective charity the mass of chronic and hopeless pauperism—represented by the *indoor* paupers, has not diminished, but has gone on steadily increasing with our increasing population and our far more rapidly increasing wealth (see Diagram III.) These facts show that the quotation of Poor Law statistics to prove the diminution of poverty and distress is a complete delusion, since they do not imply any decrease in the number of those who are unable to support life without charitable relief. But I will adduce another and distinct class of evidence to show that destitution is actually increasing. In the Registrar-General's Annual Summary of Births and Deaths in London, we find

DIAGRAM III.

Increase of Wealth, Pauperism, and Population.

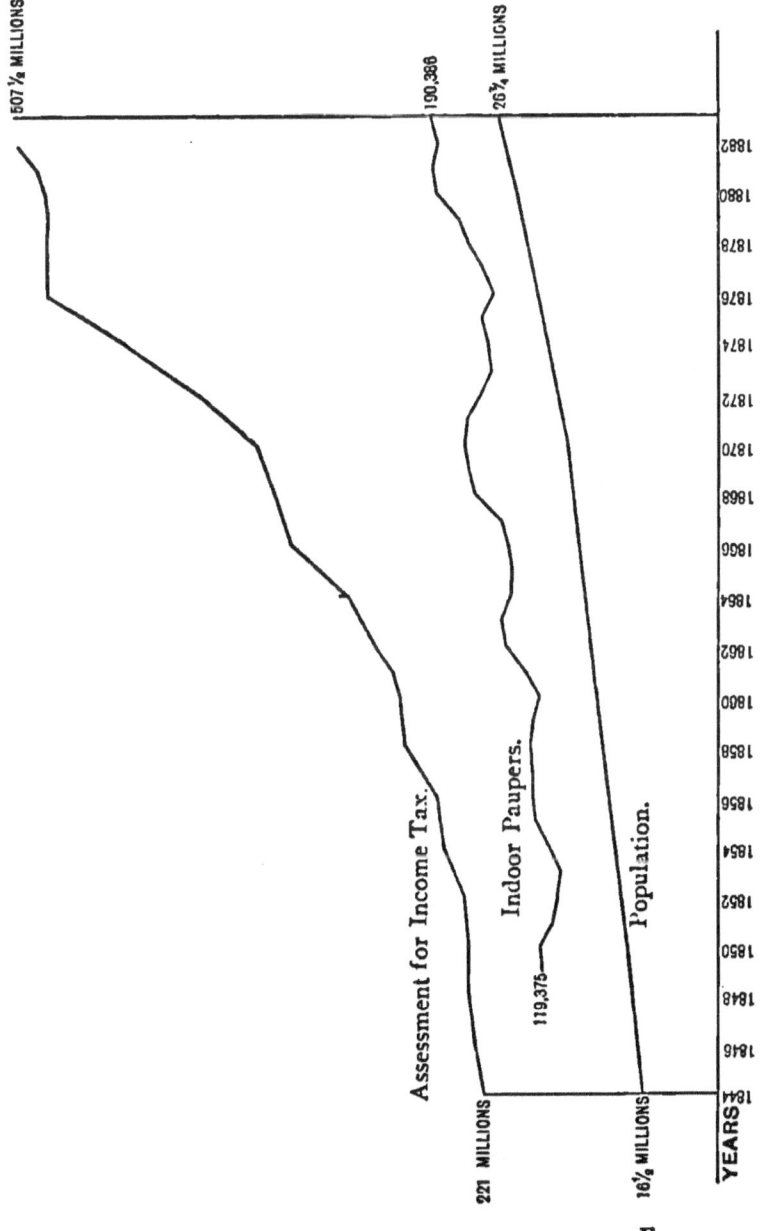

a record of the number of deaths in workhouses, hospitals, and other public institutions. If we add half the deaths in hospitals to the deaths in work-houses as fairly representing those of the destitute classes, we find them to amount, in 1872,[1] to 8,674, or **12·2** per cent. of the total deaths for that year, while in 1881 they reached 13,132, or **16·2** per cent. of the deaths.

Whence this enormous increase in deaths of the destitute classes in these public institutions, if destitution has not itself greatly increased ? The increase of 4 per cent. on the total deaths, and taking for this class of people so high a mortality as 30 per thousand living, shows that 107,000 persons have been added to the number of destitute poor in London in ten years !

Yet another independent item of evidence that destitution has increased in London during the last few years is afforded by the writer of the articles on "Poor Men's Politics" in the *Daily News*, in 1883. He states, that the payments for many kinds of work, such as match-box making, and most slop-work, have become lower and lower for several years, and although they have reached a point at which the proceeds of sixteen hours' work a day will barely support the most miserable existence, they are still falling. If these facts are correct—and many de-tailed examples are given, and have not been called

---

[1] The year 1872 is taken because 1871 was the year of the great epidemic of small-pox, when the number who died in workhouses and other hospitals was abnormally large.

in question—they prove the existence of more and
more severe competition resulting in a continuous
lowering of wages and, necessarily, in greater
poverty.

We have thus several distinct classes of facts
which all converge to demonstrate the increasing
destitution of our great cities, an increase in large
part attributable to the continued influx of the rural
populations. This destitution implies an almost
total cessation of the power of purchasing manufactured goods, and it thus constitutes one of the
most important of the causes of the prevailing
depression of trade.

The Influence of the Depopulation of Ireland.—
Another not unimportant factor of the same character
as that we have been just considering is the continued depopulation of Ireland. Since 1870 the
population of that country has diminished by nearly
half a million, but the emigration during the same
period has been about 883,000. These emigrants
are mostly adults, chiefly men in the prime of life,
and often of a rather superior class, so that they represent a loss to the country both as producers and
consumers of perhaps double the number of the
average population. The effective loss to Ireland is
therefore more nearly represented by a decreased
population of one and a-half millions than by the
half-million of actual decrease, and it is this higher
number which will best measure the loss we have
suffered in purchasers of our goods. In 1880 we
had absolute famine in Ireland; while, that there

has been a continuous increase of destitution for a long time is shown by the increase year by year of the amount expended in relief of the poor, which in 1870 was £814,445, and in 1883 reached £1,263,758, and this, be it remembered, with a declining population! These alarming facts render it certain that, for the last twelve years Ireland has been becoming poorer and poorer, and less able to consume our manufactured goods, and this has doubtless contributed in a not unimportant degree to increase the general commercial depression.

It may perhaps be objected that all this is not exceptional in Ireland—that the population has been decreasing for the last forty years, that emigration has gone on during the same period, and often more rapidly than in recent years, and that distress and destitution are there chronic. All this is no doubt true, but it does not really affect the question; for if Ireland consumes less of our goods now than she did ten years ago that is a distinct cause of depression, whether the decreased consumption had been going on during the preceding ten years or not. During periods of average prosperity we have not felt this decrease, but it has nevertheless existed; and now that our time of trouble has arrived the ever-increasing poverty of the sister isle adds materially to the burden we have to bear.

CHAPTER VIII.

THE AGRICULTURAL DEPRESSION.

ACCORDING to Sir James Caird's estimates we have had, since 1870, eleven harvests under, and only three above the average yield, while those of the four years 1875, 1876, 1877, and 1878 have been decidedly bad, the last of them so much so as to be disastrous. It is impossible to get at any correct estimate of the amount of loss suffered by farmers from these bad seasons, but in order to be able to form some conception of the probable loss during the last ten years we will make use of an estimate given in the *Times* of the yield of wheat in each year, and the area of the crop. From this we find that the ten years 1875–1884 gave 2·3 bushels an acre below the annual average, while the acreage was somewhat over three millions. This gives a loss of seventy million bushels, worth say £17,500,000, and adding an equal amount for the loss on all other grain crops less the gain on grass and green crops, which will probably be a liberal allowance, we have a total of thirty-five millions as the loss in ten years, or three and a-half millions a year. The cultivated land being about fifty millions of acres, this is equivalent to an addition of one shilling and fivepence an acre to the rent, an amount of loss which certainly ought not to have ruined the agriculturists of a wealthy country like ours if the land were held and cultivated under reasonable conditions.

Nevertheless there is the undoubted fact that thousands of farmers have been ruined, and that large areas of land have gone out of cultivation ; and Mr. W. E. Bear, in a paper read at a conference of the Farmers' Alliance in November last, stated the causes of the agricultural depression to be mainly three : (1) the great rise of rents which took place after the Russian war and during our period of maximum prosperity, and which amounted to far more than the land is really worth in ordinary times ; (2) the predominance of bad seasons; and (3) the greatly diminished prices of most agricultural produce at the same time that wages as well as local and general taxation had increased. These causes, adduced by a person of such wide experience and ample knowledge as the editor of the *Mark Lane Express*, will probably be accepted as sufficient to account for the facts ; and they are supported and enforced by the equally high authority of Professor James Thorold Rogers, M.P., who, in a letter to the *Daily News* in December last, stated, on the authority of the Reports of the Commissioners of Inland Revenue, that farmers' rents had been increased 27·3 per cent. between 1853 and 1877, while subsequent reductions had only been 9½ per cent., and remissions 4 per cent. These high rents, he assures us, absorbed much of the farmer's capital (as well as his profits), so that six years ago it was not on the average more than £6 an acre, instead of £8 or £10 which is essential to good cultivation, while at the present time it is believed to be not more than £4. It is this loss of capital and the consequent hard struggle to keep afloat that has caused so many farmers to cut down expenses by discharging labourers and diminishing their purchases of artificial manures, thus inevitably deteriorating the land, and rendering the bad seasons much more disastrous than they otherwise need have been. The Agricultural Labourers' Union has published the evidence of labourers collected in various parts of the country, and their unanimous testimony is that much less labour is employed now than ten years ago, and that there is a corresponding diminution in the produce of the land.[1]

We will now proceed to examine in some detail the chief facts connected with this branch of the question, and consider to what extent and in what manner they bear upon the main object of our inquiry.

The Agricultural Returns for Great Britain tell us that from 1873 to 1884 the quantity of arable

---

[1] *Evidence on the Cause of the present Agricultural Depression obtained from practical and* bona fide *Farm Labourers, issued by the authority of the Executive Committee of the N.A.L.U.* Leamington : Curtis and Beamish, Priory Terrace. 1880.

land in the country has decreased by considerably more than a million acres. The reason of this is, chiefly that landlords having farms thrown on their hands, and being unable to obtain fresh tenants, find it the most economical method to lay down the land in permanent pasture, which requires the minimum of labour, superintendence, and expenditure to work. This in part explains the forced exodus of the agricultural labourers no longer required to cultivate land thus laid down. But this change of land from arable to pasture, though convenient and even profitable to the landlord, is a very serious matter for the community, since it involves a great decrease in the production of food. Let us see how much we thus lose.

It is usually estimated that an acre of pasture will produce annually fifty pounds of beef or mutton, which, at an average wholesale price of 7d. a pound amounts to 29s. 2d. But an acre of land in corn crops, according to the averages given by Mr. Robert Scott Burn in *Outlines of Modern Farming*, and taking the average prices of the last ten years, is as follows :—

	£	s.	d.	
Wheat crop, with the straw . . .	10	15	0	an acre.
Barley ,, ,, . . .	6	15	0	,,
Oats ,, ,, . . .	6	2	6	,,
Potatoes	17	17	0	,,

We have thus an average produce of £10 5s. an acre, leaving a balance in favour of arable over pasture land of more than £8 15s. an acre ; and thus, when a million acres are laid down in pasture it involves a loss in food-production of eight and three quarter millions per annum. It also causes further injury by the discharge of numbers of men who are no longer required when land is thus thrown out of cultivation. About twenty-five labourers are required on an arable farm of 1,000 acres, while probably five would be ample on the same quantity of pasture; and we should thus have a diminution of twenty thousand labourers from the change of cultivation which has taken place, or, with their families, a population of sixty or eighty thousand, which from this cause alone have been obliged to quit their homes, and have mostly drifted hopelessly to the great towns. But we have suffered yet additional loss from the large number of farms which are now, and have been for some years, lying absolutely waste and uncultivated. In several counties these cover thousands of acres, and in 1881 amounted in England and Wales to 43,817 acres.[1] This cause alone must have added a not inconsiderable item to the absolute loss of wealth, and the disastrous depopulation of the rural districts.

It is the opinion of the most intelligent farmers that no such agricultural distress as now exists would have occurred had the tenant been really able to make a free contract with his landlord. But he has always been in the position of having a large amount of his capital sunk in the land, for which, in the event of his quitting his holding, he could

---

[1] These figures are given in Mr. Druce's *Report to the Duke of Richmond's Commission on Agricultural Depression*, p. 31.

obtain no adequate compensation. When, therefore, having been impoverished by losses during a succession of bad seasons, his landlord refuses to reduce the rent (although he may have made an abatement in certain years), the farmer holds on as long as possible hoping that a good season may enable him to recover himself, rather than face the almost certain ruin involved in giving up his farm and entering on a new one with insufficient capital. Mr. J. W. Barclay, M.P., an agriculturist of the highest skill and experience, states that it requires constant unremunerative expenditure for five, ten, or even more years before profitable returns can be obtained, but that when once a farm has been brought to its highest state of fertility, this can be maintained at a comparatively small outlay. But it is evident that no farmer can cultivate in this way without security of tenure, and the certainty that his rent will not be raised on account of the fertility which he himself has created; while, in order to produce the best results he must have complete freedom of action, and be released from all those harassing restrictions and covenants which almost all landlords still insist upon. With *continuity of occupancy, and fair rents fixed for long periods and never to be raised on account of improvements effected by the occupier*, Mr. Barclay is of opinion that our land is still capable of well repaying the expenditure of labour and capital in its cultivation.[1] The present

---

[1] *The Remedy for Agricultural Distress*, p. 19. Third Edition. By J. W. Barclay, M.P. London. 1880.

agricultural depression is, therefore, more distinctly
traceable to a bad land-system, than to the fact of
there having been a succession of bad seasons;
while, however caused, it has in its results impoverished farmers, pauperised labourers, and diminished the production of food, and all this on such
a vast scale as to constitute by itself a sufficient
cause for a considerable amount of commercial
depression.

Turning now to Ireland, we find that the deterioration of its agricultural condition has been
even greater than in England, and of longer continuance. Since 1860 the land under corn and
green crops has decreased by the enormous amount
of more than a million acres, and since the same
date cattle *increased* by nearly half a million, owing
to the substitution of large grazing farms for peasant
holdings, while sheep, pigs, and horses all *decreased* in
number. Within the period with which we are now
more especially concerned a still more alarming change
has occurred, considerable areas going altogether out
of cultivation and reverting to a state of nature.
Between 1872 and 1882 not only did land under
crops diminish by 291,410 acres, but land under grass
also diminished by 166,520 acres, the balance being
now made up by " bog, waste, etc," which increased
by 457,930 acres ! These facts were given by the late
Mr. Sullivan, M.P., in the *Nineteenth Century*, July,
1883, on the authority of official returns, and they
afford us a striking illustration from another point
of view, of the impoverishment of the country by

evictions and excessive rents, which compelled the
Government to attempt a remedy by the Irish Land
Act of 1881. Both by diminished population, increase of destitution, and decreased productiveness
of the soil, unhappy Ireland has contributed her
full share to swell the flowing tide of commercial
depression.

CHAPTER IX.

MILLIONAIRES A CAUSE OF DEPRESSION.

FROM 1862 to 1872 our trade and our wealth increased with the greatest rapidity, our exports having actually more than doubled in value in that short period. The chief result of this enormous commercial progress was the building up of huge fortunes such as were previously almost unknown, and a corresponding increase in the value of ground-rents owing to the rapid extension of great cities and manufacturing towns, which added immensely to the incomes of the great landowners; and this latter increase has continued, though somewhat less rapidly, down to the present time. In the twelve years 1867–79, the assessments of landed property under Schedule A. of the Income Tax increased from £110,696,900 to £147,921,687, or more than one-third; while since 1860, allowing for the change in the mode of assessment in 1867, it has almost exactly doubled.

The *New Domesday Book* shows us that in 1874 there were sixteen landowners who had each incomes of over £100,000 a year, exclusive of property in London, where the increase of value has been greatest.   At the present time probably double this number have incomes above the same limit, which, at thirty years' purchase, represents property worth three millions.   But, besides landowners, we have proof that large fortunes have greatly increased among the mercantile and financial classes.   Forty or fifty years ago a commercial millionaire was a phenomenon much talked of as something altogether exceptional and portentous.   Now, they are to be counted by scores, and excite no special remark.   In the *Financial Reform Almanack* for last year a list was given of the fortunes of a quarter of a million and upwards which had paid probate duty during the previous twenty years.   In order to ascertain whether there has been any marked recent increase I have grouped these fortunes in two series, as they belong to the first and last ten years respectively, and have also separated them into three classes according as they are under half a million, under a million, or over a million.   In the first period, 1863–1872, the fortunes above a quarter of a million were 162, in the latter period, 1873–1882, they were 208, showing an increase of more than thirty per cent.   Fortunes between a quarter and half a million had increased from 126 to 170 in number; those between half a million and a million from twenty-five to twenty-seven; and those above a million from ten to eighteen.   Thus the greatest of these fortunes, those ranging from one to three millions, have increased most rapidly in number. We must also remember that these eighteen millionaires are such in respect of personal property alone, and that if we had an account of their landed property as well, a considerable number who paid probate duty under a million would be found to rank as millionaires, and thus the number would be perhaps doubled. The actual number living at any one time cannot be known, but it is certainly more than those who die in the course of ten years.

But admitting it to be proved that very great . fortunes have proportionately increased in the last ten or fifteen years, it remains to be shown how this bears upon the question we are discussing, since wealth, in whosesoever hands it may be, is circulated and spent, and is thus often supposed to do all the good to trade and to the interests of labour that it is capable of doing. I believe, however, that this is an error, and that vast accumulations of capital in few hands can be shown to have an evil effect on trade and to be one of the causes of the present depression.

The existence of very large capitalists leads to bad results, in the first place, by rendering competition more severe and the reaction from over-trading and over-manufacture more disastrous. When the tide of prosperity is flowing and there seems no limit to the possibilities of extension in our commerce, the great capitalist increases his establishments, the size of his factories, and the number of his workmen, so as, if possible, to distance all his rivals, and secure the first place in his particular department of the markets of the world. And when the check comes and the demand for our goods diminishes, it is the great capitalist who can keep on longest, working first at a very low rate of profit, and often even at a loss, till many smaller men are ruined by the hopeless competition. He thus continues to produce till the markets are glutted, and then when the inevitable reduction of output occurs the workers are doomed to long-continued suffering. With a number of comparatively small capitalists the suffering would be less severe, because they could not afford to work at so low a rate of profit or to risk the accumulation of such large stocks, and thus production would keep more closely to the demands of the market.

But this is a comparatively small and incidental feature of few and great as opposed to many and moderate capitalists. The more essential and important consideration is this—that *whenever the few rapidly accumulate excessive wealth, the many must, necessarily, become comparatively poorer.* This is not generally acknowledged, but the proof of it is easy. Every year a definite amount of wealth is produced in our country by various kinds of industry, and the particular share of every individual is directly or indirectly, derived from this store of wealth. There is really no other means of accumulating wealth or storing up capital but by obtaining, in one way or another, a portion of this annually-produced national wealth. The landowner, by holding possession of the prime essential of existence and the fundamental

F

source of all wealth, obtains a very large share by his power of taxing the community in the form of rent. The trader gets his share in return for the labour, skill, and capital which he expends in facilitating home exchange; while the merchant secures his share for doing the same thing as regards international exchange. Every professional man receives a share from the same store of wealth in return for services rendered; the government official and the fund-holder are both paid out of the same fund contributed by the whole nation in the form of taxes, while every kind of speculation, whether in finance or trade, causes merely a change in the ownership of some of the same wealth, what one man gains some others necessarily losing. Hence the increase of millionaires involves merely a change in the distribution of the fixed store of wealth which the workers of the nation annually create, and, therefore, *many must be inevitably poorer than if these great fortunes had not been accumulated.*[1] Of course some of these fortunes are made, wholly or partially, at the expense of the people of other countries, but this does not affect the general fact, from which

---

[1] This is all implied in the opening paragraph of Adam Smith's *Wealth of Nations*, which reads thus: "The annual labour of every nation is the fund which originally supplies it with all the necessaries and conveniences of life which it annually consumes, and which consist always either in the immediate produce of that labour or in what is purchased with that produce from other nations." This fundamental principle enunciated by the father of political economy is almost entirely overlooked by modern writers in their unlimited admiration of wealth and capital.

(as John Stuart Mill said of the Law of Distribution of Profits), "resting as it does on a law of arithmetic, there is no escape."

It will no doubt be objected that the great incomes of these millionaires are all either expended by themselves, or used in the form of loans by others, and that thus the effect on trade will be the same in the end whether one person possesses the wealth or many. But this reasoning is not sound, because, even though the money may all be circulated and spent, it will be spent in a very different way in the two cases, and this is so important a point that it requires careful consideration. Let us suppose, for example, that one portion of the common store of wealth goes to provide one income of £50,000 a year, while another equal portion goes to add, on the average, £100 a year to the incomes of five hundred families of small or moderate means. In the former case a considerable portion of the money will usually be spent in pure luxury, such as horses and carriages, jewellery, ornaments, and pictures, servants, foreign travel, horse-racing, yachting, entertainments, and expensive dress, all things which give comparatively small direct employment to the great manufacturing industries of the country. In the latter case five hundred families will be raised several degrees in the scale of comfort, which means that more money will be spent by each of them on clothes, household linen, furniture, and the ordinary necessaries and comforts of life, which will all be used more freely or renewed more frequently, and which

will in the aggregate give an immensely greater
support to our home manufactures and general trade
—since our most numerous and important manufactures, which most influence our general prosperity,
are those which supply, not the extravagance and
luxury of the wealthy, but the ordinary necessaries
and simple comforts of life for the mass of the community. It cannot, therefore, be doubted that the
more wealth is diffused the more steady and constant
will be the demand for our staple manufactures, and
the more surely will the happiness of the community
be advanced.

Some indication of the effects on trade of the
undue increase of the very wealthy at the expense
of the mass of the people, is given us by comparing
the census returns of 1881 with those of 1871. We
find that the number of persons employed in many
of our great industries, which supply the common
articles of clothing and food, have either remained
stationary in proportion to the population, or have
actually declined; while those who are employed
in such industries as minister chiefly to the wants,
pleasures, or luxuries of the rich, have often dis-
proportionately increased. The growth of the general
population was **14·36** per cent., while those employed
in the cotton manufacture had increased only **6** per
cent.; and those in the linen, hosiery, woollen and
worsted manufactures had all actually declined.
Metal workers had increased in due proportion to
the population; drapers, who supply the most essential wants of the whole population, had increased in a

less ratio than population—only **7** per cent.; while milliners, who are more largely employed by the wealthy classes, had increased **18** per cent. Carpet and rug makers, depending chiefly on the well-to-do and wealthy classes, had increased **23** per cent.; gardeners, including nurserymen and florists, almost wholly patronised by the wealthy, **24** per cent; while musicians and dealers in music and musical instruments had increased **37** per cent. These few facts certainly confirm the view that.the great increase of wealth and luxury in recent times has been accompanied by, and—as has been sufficiently demonstrated—has even been a direct cause of the comparative impoverishment of our middle and lower classes, and has thus, by diminishing the consumption of the necessaries and ordinary comforts of life, contributed to bring about the prevailing depression of trade.

CHAPTER X.

OF late years there has been a very great increase of speculation, both as a profession and by the outside public with the hope of adding to their means, but it is very difficult to get at the amount of this increase, owing to changes in the classification of trades and professions at successive censuses.[1] We find it stated, however, that bankers and their clerks increased **35** per cent. in the ten years 1871-81 ; accountants increased **20** per cent.; while persons occupied in insurance increased from **5,657** in 1871 to **15,068** in 1881, but the authors of the Census Report are unable to give an explanation of this extraordinary increase. We may however conjecture that large numbers of persons who live by various modes of financial speculation, found this a convenient designation under which to return themselves, and it is perhaps for the same reason that agents or brokers have also very largely increased.

But the greatest, and I believe the most injurious,

[1] See *Census of England and Wales*, 1881, vol. iv. pp. 33, 34.

extension of speculation, has occurred in connection with the numerous public companies which have been formed under the Limited Liability Acts; and although here, too, there is difficulty in getting full and accurate information, yet sufficient facts are available to indicate the nature and extent of the evil.

A Blue Book on "Joint Stock Companies" was presented to Parliament in April, 1884, from which we learn that more than *twenty thousand* new companies have been formed under the above-named Acts, or at the rate of nearly a thousand every year. The progressive increase of these is shown if we take three equal periods of seven years each, when we find that from 1863 to 1869 there were **4,782** new limited companies; from 1870 to 1876 there were **6,905** ; and from 1877 to 1883 no less than **8,643** ; and they are still increasing, for during the last three years more had been formed than ever before in the same time, the last year, 1883, having **1,634**, the highest number yet reached. Every one knows that the great majority of these companies are not formed for the purpose of genuine trade, but merely to serve the ends of financiers, speculators, and promoters, and we accordingly find that more than *twelve thousand* of them have been officially wound up, or have otherwise ceased to exist. Out of 357 registered in the first three months of 1883, there were eighteen in liquidation before they were a year old.

The nominal capital of the companies formed in

1883 amounted to more than 167 millions, an average of about £100,000 each ; while of the eight thousand believed to be still in existence, the actual paid-up capital is stated to be over 475 millions, or on the average, £55,000 each. If, now, we suppose the twelve thousand companies which have failed to have lost the comparatively very small capital of £10,000 each, we shall have a total of 120 milions, an average loss of about six millions a year, beginning, say, with four millions and gradually increasing up to eight millions at the present time. But this is not all, for a considerable proportion of the eight thousand companies still existing are losing money, and helping to ruin numbers of their shareholders by failure of dividends or the pressure of calls.

It is well known that the class which mainly supports the numerous companies, got up either by regular financiers or enthusiastic, but untrustworthy, inventors or promoters, consists largely of persons of small property or fixed incomes, who seek to add to their means by what appears to them a perfectly safe business investment. Among these are large numbers of clergymen, country tradesmen, and professional men, single ladies and widows, and not only are the prospectuses of new companies ingeniously prepared with a view to induce such people to take shares, but they are also plied with circulars from agents and brokers offering them exceptional advantages, such as shares, which, under special circumstances, are obliged to be sold at a sacrifice. Scores of thousands of such people have been either ruined, or have had their means seriously straitened, by putting faith in these representations, and almost every one of the twelve thousand wound-up companies has brought poverty and sorrow to its hundreds or thousands of middle-class homes. If we could know the whole sad hisotry of these companies it would probably be found that no other Act of Parliament in modern times has, unintentionally, caused so much distress and suffering on the one hand, so much gambling˙and dishonesty on the other, as the much-lauded " Limited Liability Act."

Now if we consider that the thousands of families who have year by year lost money by these investments, and have often been thereby permanently impoverished, have thenceforth been obliged to economise, and that this is most easily done by making such articles as furniture, carpets, household linen, and general clothing last longer than before— since food and firing cannot be so easily reduced—it will be seen that the direct and immediate effect must be a diminished consumption of many of our staple manufactures, and hence a corresponding depression of trade. No doubt the speculators and others who gain what these people have lost spend more than before, but, not only are they fewer in number, but there is a tendency for money gained by speculation to be spent on wasteful luxuries rather than on the ordinary comforts and decencies of life ; and thus the effect is exactly the same as that which has already been shown to occur in the case of millionaires as opposed to people of moderate incomes.

It is singular that an Act which was strongly advocated by John Stuart Mill, and by political economists generally, should have produced such disastrous effects, and, so far as we can see, so little counterbalancing good. It never seems to have been foreseen that it would give birth to an extensive class of men who would make it their special study to get up worthless but attractive companies, and to induce the needy and credulous public to invest their money, with the hope of participating in the supposed large and certain profits of genuine industrial operations. Yet the Act was evidently intended to enable people to obtain such benefits; and the lesson we should learn from the result seems to be, that all investments should be discouraged except those in which the investor has either a personal knowledge of the business carried on, and an opportunity of intelligently watching its progress, or an equally personal knowledge of the acting partners in the concern, and an assured conviction both of their capability and their integrity. The old law of unlimited liability of partners tended to restrict industrial partnerships to such cases; the new law acted as an invitation to every one to join in them, although totally ignorant both of the business to be carried on and of the ability and character of the men who had the management of it ; and the result has been the establishment of a new form of

gambling on a gigantic scale and under the protection of the law, which, like all other gambling, has
brought gain to the initiated few, loss to the ignorant
and credulous multitude.

The great evil of such legislative mistakes is, that
it is so exceedingly difficult to remedy them. Great
vested interests are created by them which oppose all
change; and in this case there have arisen special
classes of lawyers, accountants, directors, and promoters, to whom the creation and the winding-up of
companies afford a comfortable subsistence. Moreover, the sufferers are too widespread, too disconnected, and often too much ashamed of their losses
to take any common action, and thus the law will
probably remain unrepealed, and continue perhaps
for generation after generation to immolate its crowds
of victims.

CHAPTER XI.

COMPLAINTS are often made that English manufactures have of late years deteriorated in quality, and that, in consequence, certain classes of them have been displaced by those of other countries in colonial and foreign markets, and hence has resulted a certain amount of injury to our trade. There seems to be considerable truth in these allegations, but here, more than in any other branch of our subject, it is difficult to form any trustworthy estimate of the extent of the evil.

The chief articles to which these remarks apply are our woollen and cotton goods, and also to some of our silks and hardware. Our woollen cloths are largely adulterated with refuse materials worked up into "shoddy," and the extent of the adulteration may be judged by the fact that forty millions of pounds of this material are made annually in Yorkshire. The skill with which shoddy is incorporated with wool so as to produce goods of apparently high quality, is such, that the adulteration is with difficulty detected, and it is alleged that it is often used in goods which are sold by the manufacturer as being "all wool."

In cottons and calicoes the adulteration is still more serious. Previous to 1854 flour paste and tallow were used to give stiffness and weight to inferior goods, and 20 per cent. of these materials were often used. The Russian war making tallow dear, a substitute was found in china-clay and size, which has since entirely supplanted the earlier form of "dressing." At the time of the American civil war in 1862 cotton became abnormally dear, and this was a temptation to increase the use of the dressing material to the utmost. By means of chloride of magnesia the china-clay is kept permanently damp, and thus a greater quantity can be held by the cotton, and it is stated that from 50 to 90 per cent. of these materials is now contained in some qualities of what is still termed "calico." In order to make this adhere to the threads during the process of weaving the atmosphere has to be kept charged with moisture to such an extent as to saturate the clothes of the workmen, to the serious injury of their health and actual increase of their rate of mortality.[1]

These distressing facts have been brought to the notice of Parliament, but no word of reprobation appears to have been spoken against them. The statement of the manufacturers that there was "a demand for such goods," was considered conclusive. Would a "demand" for electro-plated dollars of

[1] Most of the facts are given in the article "Adulteration" in the new edition of the *Encyclopædia Britannica*.

base metal to be disposed of in eastern countries be considered equally to justify that manufacture ? For it will, I believe, be found on inquiry that these sham calicoes are only disposed of in countries where they serve the purpose of money, all important payments, whether for labour or for goods, being made in fathoms or pieces of cloth; and the people, having always been accustomed to take them, are obliged to submit to the gradual deterioration. There is assuredly no real *demand* for goods which cannot be washed or even wetted without becoming worthless, except by the intermediate merchants and traders who are ever seeking to rival each other in the superior cheapness of what appear to be similar articles. Although these commonest and worst of calicoes are only accepted by barbarous people who can get no other, yet adulteration of the same kind, though less in degree, prevails in much higher qualities, with the result that American cottons are in many markets greatly preferred to those of English make.

Silk is also adulterated with jute, and weighted with dye-stuffs, so that in black or brown silks half the weight is sometimes due to extraneous matter.

I am able to give a few facts as to actual results of this adulteration on our colonial trade on the authority of Dr. Fisher, of Canterbury, New Zealand, who has resided in that colony for thirty years. He informs me that, being disgusted with the "shoddy" sent out to them from England, under the mistaken notion that "anything was good enough for the colonies," the New Zealanders determined many years ago to manufacture their own wool, and went to much trouble and expense to do so; and they now make a variety of woollen goods which not only have an extensive sale in the colonies, but are even being sent to England, having the reputation of a thoroughly genuine article. Some of the Australian colonies have also extensive woollen factories, which were probably first established for the same reason as in New Zealand. The Sheffield hardware exported to the colonies has long been so bad that it is now almost wholly superseded by American goods, which are said to be much superior, and I am informed by two separate authorities that no colonial workman will use an English tool if he can get one of American manufacture. American cottons are also generally preferred to ours in the colonies.

There can then, I think, be little doubt that the comparatively recent extension of the various modes of adulteration and inferiority of manufacture above referred to, have, to some extent, prejudicially affected our reputation as honest manufacturers and diminished the demand for our goods; but as there are no means of ascertaining the amount of injury thus done we are not at present justified in imputing any considerable part of the existing depression of trade to causes of this nature.

CHAPTER XII.

HAVING thus passed in review the chief causes which have brought about the present depression of trade, it may be well to point out that the most important of them apply with equal, and sometimes even with greater, force to other countries than our own, and we thus have explained the remarkable fact that the depression has extended, almost simultaneously, over the whole of the great civilised States of the world. The number of the men employed either as soldiers or in the various occupations connected with the equipment of an army and navy, has increased more rapidly in France, Russia, and Italy, than with us, and this will explain the exceptional severity of the distress in those countries. America does not now suffer from this cause : but nowhere in the world have colossal fortunes, rabid speculation, and great monopolies reached so portentous a magnitude, or exerted so pernicious an influence. America also suffers under a burden of municipal debt far beyond any other country. A

recent American newspaper gives a comparative
statement of the debt of their chief cities as compared with ours, as follows :—

	Average Taxation per Head.	Municipal Debt.
14 Great American Cities . . .	$14·18 . . .	$41·56
14 Great English Towns . . .	$7·52 . . .	$21·56

showing that, whether as regards municipal taxation
or municipal debts America suffers twice as much as
we do. But this is not all. The smaller towns in
England have either very little debt or are wholly
free from it, while in America it is stated that the
small towns are the most heavily in debt, and that in
some cases it reaches from $100 to over $200 per
head. When we remember the revelations as to the
organised plunder that went on for years by the
ring which had monopolised the municipal government of New York, we may fairly assume that a
considerable portion of the municipal debts of
America do not represent useful public works or
reproductive expenditure, but have largely been
wasted in various forms of jobbery. Adding this
burden to the heavy State taxation; taking into
account the exorbitant prices of most of the necessaries of life due to the protective system; the wide
prevalence of speculation not only on the Stock
Exchange but as manifested by the " rings" and
"corners" in every department of commerce; the
huge railroad monopolies, and the colossal fortunes
of American millionaires; we have ample reasons

G

why the depression should have been felt in America as severely as by us.

We must also remember that all the great manufacturing nations alike suffer from the impoverishment caused by each of them, whether this occurs among their own subjects, or among those of the countries which are devastated by war or oppressed by taxation in order to pay interest on the loans obtained by their despotic rulers—and this because modern manufacturers find customers for their goods in almost every country in the world.

All too suffer under bad land systems, large areas being everywhere monopolised by a few owners, while the labourers have hardly ever that general opportunity of acquiring a plot of land which both renders them better off by enabling them to utilise all their spare hours, and at the same time has a tendency to raise the rate of wages by making them less absolutely dependent on their employers. Even where there are numerous peasant-proprietors, the benefits of the system are often neutralised by the fact that their lands are heavily mortgaged; while in many cases the farms are so scattered—a few acres often consisting of scores of disconnected, unfenced plots, some of them a mile or more apart—that any approach to good or economical cultivation is impossible—a wretched system which largely prevails both in France and Germany. It is therefore clear that the wide extension of the area of the depression, which has caused so much difficulty to those who have endeavoured to explain it by causes peculiar to our own country, affords of itself a strong argument in favour of the explanation here given, inasmuch as the various causes to the combined action of which it is imputed, either exist in considerable force in all the great manufacturing countries of the world, or are of such a nature as equally to affect the trade of all these countries.

Much has been said as to the blessings of commerce among nations. It is, however, equally true that it causes the sufferings of each to be felt by all, and renders each nation responsible, not only morally but in material results, for the injustice and oppression that impoverishes the inhabitants of any country with which it trades. The ties of commerce unite nations alike for good and evil, and render the prosperity of each dependent on the equal prosperity of all the rest. When this great truth is well understood it may perhaps become the peace-maker of the world.

PART II.

REMEDIES.

CHAPTER XIII.

FINANCIAL AND COMMERCIAL REMEDIES.

HAVING traced to their several sources the many and often complex causes which have combined to produce the present depression of trade, it is not difficult to see the nature of the remedies required, though it may not always be easy to apply them in practice. Much will depend on a clear appreciation of the problem by the people at large, and a determination that the errors of the past shall not be repeated in the future; and something may be at once effected by judicious legislation. Let us then see what are the remedies suggested by the various causes which have contributed to produce the disease.

Foreign Loans.—Taking first the case of the enormous foreign loans, mostly to despotic rulers, it is clear that they cannot be directly forbidden, but it is none the less clear that they can be discountenanced by public opinion, and ignored or discouraged by the Government.   When it is once admitted that such loans are essentially immoral in their nature, because they enable despotic rulers to gratify their passions, their follies, or even their vices at the expense of their subjects, we shall not permit our Government to interfere in any way when the overburdened people seek to throw off their yoke; and when that is known, financiers and capitalists will no longer risk their money on such bad security.

The evil results of these loans consist essentially in the fact that whole nations are impoverished by being forced to pay interest for money they have either never received, or have in no way benefited by, and in the borrowing of which they were not consulted.   The money was lent with the full knowledge that there was no security beyond the continuance of the despot's power.   It was therefore lent on oppressive terms, and at usurious rates of interest, and it is absolutely unjust that, when any of these down-trodden peoples seek to rid themselves of their oppressor, he should be assisted by the governments of the lenders to put down their justifiable rebellion. It is often alleged or intimated that it is in the interests of *honesty,* of the payment of debts justly due, that we interfere in such cases; but this is a strange confusion of ideas.   It is dishonest not to pay a debt you have yourself incurred, but it is not dishonest to refuse to pay one which was incurred in

your name but without your authority, and not even
for your benefit. The dishonesty lies with those who
use force to compel you to pay another's debt against
your will. It should always be remembered that
when money is lent on such terms as above indicated,
the probability of the cessation of the interest and
loss of the capital is one of the known conditions
of the bargain, *and is discounted in the high interest
and low price of issue.* When, therefore, any outside
governments interfere to support one of these despotic borrowers against their subjects, they are simply
robbing an oppressed community for the benefit of a
few usurers and speculators, and to the injury of their
own people, for *they thus help to perpetuate the depression of trade which is largely due to the poverty of these
same over-taxed nations.*

When these facts are clearly perceived, and their
consequences fully appreciated, perhaps self-interest
will do what the love of justice and of freedom have
not alone been able to effect, and the people of this
country will insist that, instead of helping to repress
the rebellion of oppressed nations against their op-
pressors, our rulers shall in every case give them at
least our moral support, and shall also use their influence to prevent other governments from interfering
with them. This, at all events, is clear : so long as
numerous populations are ground into poverty by
unjust and oppressive taxation they cannot be good
customers to us. Our commercial prosperity rests
upon the well-being of peoples, not on the wealth
and luxury of despots.

War Expenditure.— Closely connected with the question of foreign loans is that of the gigantic war expenditure, and repeated wars which have more or less impoverished all the chief nations of Europe, since in most cases the latter are only rendered possible by fresh loans and increased burdens on the people. At present any important alleviation of these burdens seems hopeless.

A step will be gained, however, if the working classes can be brought to see clearly how much they suffer from those huge armaments which suck the very life-blood of a nation. They will then, perhaps, when they have political power in their hands, insist that our own armament shall be strictly confined within the limits needful for self-defence, and that we shall on no pretence whatever send our armies to invade another country, or our ships to bombard its cities, *unless we are first attacked.* The only case in which a foreign war would be morally justifiable, would be that in which we gave assistance to a people struggling for freedom, or to a weak nation when unjustly attacked by a more powerful one; and these are the very cases in which we should reap the natural reward of good actions in the benefit to our trade from the increased prosperity of free and progressive communities; yet, as a matter of fact, *we never make war in so good a cause.*

The Concentration of Capital.—The excessive concentration of capital, the bad effects of which on trade have been already pointed out, may be somewhat counteracted by various social developments or it may be attacked by special legislation. The building up of great fortunes is evidently facilitated by the almost unlimited command of labour which the capitalist possesses, by the facilities for temporarily investing large sums in the numerous Government Stocks and those of great industrial companies, and by the comparative instability of the smaller competing capitalists who are largely trading on credit. Anything which betters the condition of the workers and makes them more independent of employers will check, to some extent, the capitalist's unlimited command of labour; while the conversion of all Government funds into terminable annuities, and some legislation which would greatly discourage trading on credit, would still further check the process of individual accumulation.

But, so soon as it is generally seen and admitted that excessive fortunes are not only morally hurtful to the possessors and their expectant heirs, but also have a deleterious influence on the well-being of the whole community, it will be easy to check them by absorbing for the use of the State (by means of a carefully graduated tax) all income above a certain amount, and by limiting in like manner the wealth which any individual may transmit to private persons by will or intestacy.

Extension of Speculation.—This might be very usefully checked by requiring that every transaction whatever, whether on the Stock Exchange or in commercial markets, shall pay a substantial stamp-duty on the nominal amount transferred.   This might be so graduated as not to press unduly on genuine sales and purchases, while it would seriously check all mere speculative purchases and time-bargains, and would at the same time bring in a very large amount of revenue.

The greatest relief, however, and that which would most benefit the general trade of the country, would be afforded by the total repeal of the Limited Liability Acts, which, as has been shown, are a constantly acting cause of the impoverishment of large numbers of the very classes which supply the best customers for our home manufactures.

Adulteration and Dishonesty in Manufactures.— These can probably only be dealt with by insisting that the actual composition of all manufactured goods shall be clearly stated on the goods themselves, wherever practicable, otherwise on a conspicuous label, on the principle which is already applied to coffee and spirits.   Bales of goods, marked *"Fine Calico: containing cotton* 10 *per cent., China-clay, lime, and size,* 90 *per cent.,"* or *" Rich Silk, consisting of, silk* 50 *per cent., dye-stuff* 50 *per cent."* would, no doubt, soon cease to be asked for or made.

But if such a law is to have any real effect it must be energetically enforced, and for this purpose all the respectable firms in each class of manufacture, such as cotton, wool, linen, or metal-work, should organise themselves into guilds or unions, having each a special trade-mark, which shall be an absolute guarantee that the goods bearing it are exactly what they purport to be. Such common statements as "best quality," "superfine," and "warranted all wool," will no longer be applied to goods which can only be truly characterised as "inferior quality," "coarse," and "half shoddy;" the widths and lengths specified must correspond accurately with the actual measures instead of being, as now, usually in excess of the real amounts; while dyes will not be declared "fast" when the colours will begin to run on exposure to a shower of rain. These guilds would be able to enforce the law and see that all mixtures and adulterations were openly declared to be such. Honest manufacturers would then get the full benefit of the quality of their goods, and not be subjected to the competition of adulterated articles finished so as to imitate those of the best quality. It would then be seen whether there really is "a demand" for worthless goods; while those who continue to purchase them will have no reason to complain. The proposal here made is only what common honesty dictates, and it would completely get rid of this disreputable cause of depression of trade.

CHAPTER XIV

THE REMEDY FOR AGRICULTURAL DEPRESSION.

WE now come to the most important part of our subject from the remedial point of view—that which relates to agricultural depression and the depopulation of the rural districts, because it is here that legislation can act directly and effectually to bring about a more healthy state of things. We will first consider the question as it regards the farmer and the conditions under which the present depression has arisen.

The reports of the various Assistant Commissioners to the Royal Commission on Agriculture bear out the statement that, besides bad seasons, the depression is very largely due to too high rents; and one of them remarks: "I do not think it would be difficult to show that the impoverished and beggared condition of farms which have been given up by tenants on some estates, and which are now unlet, is due to the ill-advised attempt of the landlords to get an extreme rent for their land." Other causes adduced in these reports are, increased cost of labour, want of security for the tenant's improvements, and want of freedom

in cultivation. It is also clearly brought out that
farmers are best off, and suffer least from depression,
on the largest estates, on which changes of tenants
rarely occur, rents are seldom raised, and there is the
greatest feeling of security.   Change of ownership
is dreaded by the farmer, because it often brings new
modes of management, and, not unfrequently, enhanced rents. In these respects entailed estates have
no disadvantage as compared with those under
absolute ownership, since, if under the former there
is less disposition to lay out money on improvements,
the farmer is willing to do so himself under the
feeling of security produced by continuity of ownership in the same family.[1] It is therefore evident that
the usual panacea of land-law reformers—the abolition
of entails and settlements and the greatest possible
freedom of sale—would be rather prejudicial to the
farmer than otherwise, since it would lead to numerous
changes of ownership and to the purchase of estates
by commercial men, who would at once screw up
rents to their highest pitch and thus keep the farmer
always poor ; and all the evidence goes to show that
this would be the most injurious thing possible for
agriculture.

   The classes of farmers who have succeeded best
and have not suffered under the prevailing depression
are—(1) those at moderate rents and with a practi-
cally secure tenure ; (2) those who own their own
land, or have long leases, with a sufficiency of capital

   [1] See Mr. Little's *Report on Devon, Cornwall, Dorset and Somerset*,
p. 57, col. 1.

to work it; (3) peasant-farmers who work their land with the assistance of their families, *and have not mortgaged their farms.*

Of the first class there are numerous examples on most of the great hereditary estates. Of the second, the most interesting is Mr. Prout, of Sawbridge-worth, who, on a farm of his own of 450 acres has carried on a special system of high farming with consecutive grain crops, such as no landlord would ever permit; and after full allowance for every expense of rent, interest on capital, depreciation of buildings and machinery, and cost of superintendence, has obtained a clear profit of nearly a thousand a year for the thirteen consecutive years 1866–1878, followed by a loss of less than £700 in the two years 1879–1880. At the same time the farm is actually improved in quality. The important point here to be noticed is, not so much the successful farming, though this is very remarkable, as the possibility of trying new methods of husbandry adapted to special conditions of soil, &c., which the system of landlord and tenant renders impossible.

As illustrations of peasant-farmers we may give the testimony of Mr. F. Winn Knight, M.P., of Exmoor, who states that he has sixteen tenants paying him rents from £13 up to £200 a year, *all of whom had been agricultural labourers,* and he adds— "and these rents are without any arrears and paid regularly to the last shilling." [1]

[1] See, for futher particulars of these men, Mr. Little's *Report,* p. 21.

Another case is that of Mr. George Leece, who was a farm-labourer and now has a farm in Lancashire of sixty-eight acres, mostly grass, all the labour on which is done by himself and his family. He pays a full rent, and had not suffered even in the bad years 1879–1880, and Mr. Coleman remarks: " This was a very interesting and typical case. Here was a man standing at a high rent and yet doing well mainly because his outlay was small and the labour was all done without actual cash payments, and by those whose interest it was to make the most of their time." [1]

None of the legislation yet proposed, although often complex, and difficult in working, meets all the essential requirements of the case; but the prosperity of our agriculture is far too important a matter to the whole community to be left any longer at the mercy of a system which has so manifestly broken down; and some important information is given in these Reports of the Agricultural Commission which may perhaps suggest the basis of a reform by which all parties will be equally benefited.

Details furnished by the agents of several large estates show that the costs of agency, repairs, and improvements usually amount to from 25 to 35 per cent. on the gross rental, while during some years of the depression they have been very much higher owing to abatements of rent. The management expenses seem to vary from 4 to 8 per cent. in

---

[1] Mr. Coleman's *Reports on Northumberland, Lancashire, and Cheshire*, p. 41.

ordinary years.[1] These latter expenses may be
wholly saved under a better system, while it is quite
certain that the costs of repairs and improvements
on a great estate are generally much beyond their
value to the tenant. This must inevitably be the
case whenever the persons who spend money have
no interest in economy, but rather the reverse. It
is well known to be the case in all Government expenditure of the same nature; and when agents,
solicitors, surveyors, and architects all have a hand
in the laying out of money, anything like strict
economy is almost impossible. As an illustrative
case I may mention that a friend, who holds an
official appointment and lives in a house provided
by Government, complained to me recently that he
had been much inconvenienced by having all the
window frames of his house taken out and new ones
put in. The official surveyor on his periodical in-
spection had condemned them as unsound, although
my friend, who lived in the house, had found no
fault with any of them. If this house had belonged
to my friend the window frames would have certainly
done duty for some years longer, and then, perhaps,
have been repaired at the cost of one of the new
ones. In like manner, if a farmer was the owner of
the buildings, drains, and other improvements on
his farm, he would make exactly what repairs, altera-
tions, and additions were required from time to time,

---

[1] See Mr. Druce's *Report on the Midland Counties*, pp. 10, 20, 71,
and 89 ; also Mr. Little's *Report on Devon, Cornwall, Dorset and
Somerset*, p. 52.

and no more; he would not need the assistance of either lawyer or architect in the work, which he would carry out in the most economical manner, and would thus, in all probability, save half of what is now spent, and perhaps obtain a result of more real value agriculturally than that derived from the greater outlay of the landlord.

But if one half of the 30 per cent. now expended by landlords on management and improvements can be saved, this would afford the means of enabling the tenant, *without any increase of rent*, to purchase the buildings and all the other landlord's improvements on his farm, by means of a terminable rental like those adopted under the Irish Church Act, the permanent rent being that for the value of the bare land without any improvements whatever. With a farm held under these conditions there would be no excuse for any "management," or for any interference with the tenant's complete freedom of cultivation, because he would himself be the owner of a valuable portion of the farm—that termed in Ireland the "tenant right,"—his rent would be fixed for a long term (and would then only be raised by public valuation if land generally rose in value independent of all improvements on it), and any depreciation of the holding by bad farming would be his own loss, since the selling value of his "tenant-right" would be thereby diminished. By this plan the farmer would obtain the most absolute security both of his tenure and for his improvements, he would be free to carry out any system of husbandry which he thought would be ultimately most profitable, and in many cases he would increase the fertility of the soil to an extent which would be impossible under. the present system of uncertain tenure and restrictions on cultivation : and all this would be effected in the simplest manner, without any one sacrificing a penny, but by means of savings effected in the present wasteful system of ."management" by agents and of money expended by those who are not most interested in its economical application.

Mr. J. W. Barclay, M.P., in his pamphlet, *The Remedy for Agricultural Distress*, is very clear on the point that nothing less than what is here proposed to be secured to the farmer will effectually preserve British agriculture. He says: "The cultivator of the soil *must have continuity of occupation* —that is, hold the land in perpetuity so long as he pays such fixed rent as may be agreed on." And again he says: "Peasant proprietorship, or properly, proprietorship of land by its cultivator, is the natural system of land tenure, whether considered abstractedly or by the results. In recent years the late Mr. Kay, and many others, have certified, from close observation, the superior cultivation and productiveness which attend the occupancy of land with continuity of possession, as compared with limited tenancy. But the fact was noted and commented on a century ago by that shrewd observer Arthur Young. Strongly prejudiced as he was in favour of large farms and the English system of land-tenure, he could not help being deeply impressed by the high

H

degree of cultivation which accompanied perpetuity
of tenure by the cultivator, and he has summed up
in one pregnant sentence the results of the two forms
of tenure. 'Give a man,' says he, 'the secure possession of a bleak rock, and he will turn it into a
garden; give him a nine years' lease of a garden,
and he will convert it into a desert.' But a perpetual
lease at a fixed rent is peasant-proprietorship, as was
pointed out by John Stuart Mill in his *Political
Economy*. The tenant in perpetuity has all the
advantages of absolute ownership so far as concerns
the cultivation and improvement of his holding. He
knows and feels that the fruits of his labour, be they
great or small, will be his, and that his homestead
will be his home so long as he pays the stipulated
rent." Mr. Barclay goes on to show that absolute
ownership would be worse than secure tenancy, *unless mortgaging were absolutely forbidden ;* while it is
far better for a farmer to have the use of his capital
in order to cultivate as highly as possible than to
have it tied up in the fee-simple of the land.

Now this system of secure tenancy, with ownership
of all that has been put upon or into the land, can be
secured by an arrangement such as I have here
sketched out, and would be equally advantageous to
all the parties concerned. To the landlord it would
secure a permanent income from his estate without
risk or trouble ; to the tenant all the advantages of
ownership without the capital required to purchase ;
and to the community the advantage of a progressive
agriculture unchecked by the deleterious influences of

estate-rules, shackled cultivation and conflicting interests, together with the increased employment of
labour and production of wealth which such freedom
tends to produce. No doubt landlords will be somewhat unwilling to relinquish the political power and
personal influence which attaches to the existing
system of tenure, but the country has too much at
stake to allow such objections to have much weight.
The new tenure must be generally established either
by voluntary agreements duly registered by a Land
Court, or by compulsory arrangements on the application of tenants or intending tenants. The
present time is exceptionally favourable for such
legislation, since so many landowners have suffered
from the existing depression; while it is very probable that, unless something really effectual is soon
done, future parliaments may apply even more
drastic remedies rather than allow the land to fall
out of cultivation, and one of the greatest and most
important of our industries to be ruined by a system
which has had a long trial and has landed us in
disaster.

CHAPTER XV.

THROUGHOUT the Reports of the Agricultural Commission we meet with repeated complaints by the farmers of the increased cost of labour, due, not so much to the higher wages, which all admit are none too much for the labourer to live upon, as to the inferiority of the work. This is imputed partly to the use of machinery, and partly to the boys being sent to school and so losing the early training they used to get upon the farm; but it is also largely due to the fact that many of the young and energetic labourers have left the rural districts in the hopes of bettering their condition, while education and political enlightment have naturally made labourers discontented with a position in which a life of hard work and the very poorest living has no hope to cheer it but the gloomy prospect of the workhouse.

There is, however, one sure and certain way of giving the labourer hope, of improving his condition, of making him a better workman, and keeping him

THE REMEDY FOR RURAL DEPOPULATION.   101

in his native place, and that is to let him have as
much land attached to his cottage as he can cultivate in his spare time. Wherever this is fairly tried
it never fails; and, considering how simple is the
remedy, how much it is a matter of justice as well
as good policy, it is sad to wade through the replies
to questions in the "Reports" and note how seldom
has anything been done to enable the labourer
to raise himself above the dead level of the prospective pauper. No doubt allotments are not
uncommon, and most farmers and landlords seem to
think that this is all a labourer wants or should be
allowed to have. But this is a great mistake. An
allotment is undoubtedly some benefit to a labourer,
but, comparatively a small one. It affords him no
hope; it does not open to him the realisation of that
dream of the peasant's life—a homestead of his very
own; it is in some respects positively cruel, inasmuch
as it compels him to waste much time and strength
which are most precious to him, and which might be
all saved. It is necessary to dwell somewhat on this
point because even now our most advanced politicians
are proposing to empower local authorities to purchase land in order to give labourers allotments.
But the term "allotments" has a very definite
meaning in English rural economy. It means a
a field or fields cut up into small plots of one-eighth
or a quarter of an acre, rarely of half an acre, let out
to labourers on a yearly tenure, with no security
and with the absolute prohibition of building upon
them. It is this allotment system which J. S. Mill

absolutely condemns in his *Political Economy*[1] as
being identical in principle with the old parish
allowances, and, like them, having a tendency to keep
down the rate of wages.   If this kind of tenure is
not meant the term allotment should not be used ;
but I fear it is used in ignorance of the crying
defects of the allotment system, some of which I
will endeavour to point out.

An allotment field usually is, and must necessarily
be, at a considerable distance from the cottages of
most of the labourers in a parish.   When the man
comes home to dinner the half hour he might give
to it is wasted.   In the spring or autumn the precious
half or quarter hours of twilight are wasted.   The
spare minutes of his wife and children between
household work or school hours are all wasted.   The
sewage and house refuse, which might often double
the produce of the land, are wasted, or can only be
applied to it by the expenditure of much extra toil.
Every hour of labour on the allotment may involve
an extra mile of walking, every tool and every article
of produce has to be carried to and fro.   Surely it is
more than mere cruelty, it is a social blunder—a
political crime, to compel tens of thousands of our
working men, whose time and labour are their sole
wealth, thus painfully to waste time and labour
which might be so easily saved by invariably per-
mitting them *to have land attached to their cottages, or
land on which they may build a cottage.*   By doing
this we should not only better *their* condition, not

[1] See Book II. chap. xii. par. 4, p. 223, of People's Edition.

only give *them* hope and energy and independence, but should add materially to the general store of wealth and to the very same extent benefit trade.

Allotments are now rarely allowed to be more than one-eighth or a quarter of an acre because, it is said, a man cannot cultivate more in his spare time. But though this may be true when more than half his spare time is wasted in the manner indicated above, there is abundant evidence to prove that he can, and often does, cultivate an acre, or even several acres, in his over-time when it is attached to his cottage ; and he is then able to utilise part of the land in growing fruit or other choice crops, which he can never do on an open unprotected allotment. In every case where men are allowed to have land in this way, with any approach to security of tenure, the results are strikingly beneficial, to the men themselves, to the farmers for whom they are always ready to work when required for good wages, and to the community for which they create a much larger quantity of food than the farmer can produce from the same land. A few illustrations must be given in proof of these assertions, but it would require a separate essay to do the subject justice.

It was proved before the Women's and Children's Employment Commission, in 1868, that cottagers obtained an average return from allotments of 16*l.* an acre above the farm rent. This, however, is much below what is often obtained now. Quite recently Lord Carrington stated (as already referred to at p. 44) that his 800 allotment tenants round

High Wycombe obtained a nett produce of 40*l*. an acre, while the most that a farmer can obtain from the same land by plough cultivation is 7*l*. an acre. Here is a gain to the country of 33*l*. an acre on land let in allotments over the same land in farms; and this is all clear gain, for it is produced by means of labour which would otherwise be wasted. It is produced, too, under the disadvantageous conditions which have been just pointed out, so that the benefit to the labourer himself cannot be nearly so great as if he had the land attached to his dwelling and on a permanent instead of on a yearly tenure. And yet we are repeatedly and persistently told that the *petite culture* does not pay so well as large farms! But we have yet further evidence and of a still more interesting character.

The beneficial effect of allowing labourers to have land on which to keep a cow are thus stated in Mr. Coleman's Report on Cheshire: "If Lord Tollemache's practice of letting each cottager have sufficient land to keep a cow were more generally adopted in the country, there would be less complaints, both as to the quality of labour and the difficulty of getting servants to milk. The labourer's children under such circumstances are brought up to take an interest in stock, they milk, make butter, and learn much that is useful. The skim milk is of great value as food, and the possession of a cow gives a man an interest in his home, which helps very much to keep good men from roving." And a special correspondent of the *Daily*

News says of the same estate: "The tenant-farmers, instead of objecting to the cottagers keeping a cow, are loud in praise of the system. Thanks to it they are able to secure the very pick of agricultural labourers. It is not favourable to the breeding of worthless drones. Cottages are never empty, and for that matter neither do farms go a begging. In the time of the worst depression there were always a number of applications for any farm that was likely to be vacated."

A remarkable instance of the value of land to any kind of labourers, and of the amount of capital and labour they are willing to invest in it, even without security of tenure, is afforded by the case of Penstrasse Moor, in Cornwall, the property of Sir T. Dyke Acland, which has been reported on by Mr. Little. The moor was formerly a barren waste, 500 acres of which have now been inclosed and reclaimed by miners, mechanics, or other labourers, on the security of leases for three lives at a low rent, with the custom of giving renewals by adding a fresh life when one fails, on payment of a fine. The estates thus created vary from three or four acres up to ten, and, in a few cases, twenty acres. Good houses have been built on most of the lots, and the inclosure and reclamation alone is estimated to have cost at least 6*l.* an acre. The gross produce of the land, mostly in pasture, is estimated to be more than 10*l.* an acre, which is nearly twice the average of the county. On these interesting little farms the Assistant-Commissioner remarks as follows: "Those

who work in mines work alternately in day and
night shifts, and they utilise their spare hours on
their farm; the wife and children, however, do most
of the farm work. The family have a much more
comfortable home, and many advantages, such as
milk, butter, eggs, which they would not otherwise
enjoy. The man has a motive for saving his money
and employing his spare time, and if he does not
gain a large profit as a farmer, he enjoys a position
of independence; he is elevated in the social scale;
his self-respect is awakened and stimulated, and he
acquires a stake and an interest in the country." Of
course these numerous advantages would be increased
if he had *all* the fruits of his labour secured to him,
as in justice they ought to be, instead of becoming
ultimately the property of the landlord, and only
being temporarily saved from confiscation by the
payment of repeated fines; yet the example is none
the less instructive, and Mr. Little has evidently
been greatly impressed by it, as he again returns to
the subject and makes the following observations,
which are of such vital importance to the question
we are considering, that they must be quoted in full.
He says :—

"Interesting as this subject is in its relation to
agriculture, as showing the capacity for improvement
which some barren spots possess, and as a triumph
of patience and industry, it is most valuable as an
instance where the opportunity of investing surplus
wages and spare hours in the acquirement of a home
for the family, an independent position for the

labourer, a provision for wife and children in the future, has been a great encouragement to thrift and providence. It is not only that the estate represents so much land reclaimed from the waste and put to a good use, it represents so much time well spent, which would, without this incentive, have most probably been wasted; and wages which would otherwise probably have been squandered, employed in securing a homestead and some support for the widow and family when the workman dies. I would ask, are there not many places where the same thing might be done if the opportunity were offered? Every thoughtful employer of labourers who has ever attempted to impress upon his workmen the duty of saving must have experienced a difficulty in suggesting to them an object which will appeal with sufficient force to the imagination and sentiment to overcome the habit of spending all that is earned."

Yet one more example must be given of the beneficial effects of enabling labourers to have land other than allotments. The Hon. Geo. C. Brodrick, in his valuable work *English Land and English Landlords*, gives an account of the Annandale Estate in Dumfriesshire, where farm-labourers were allowed to have leases for twenty-five years, at ordinary farm rents, of from two to six acres of land situated on roadsides, and who built their own cottages with stone and timber supplied by the landlord. "All the work on these little farms was done at by-hours,

---

[1] Royal Commission on Agriculture. Mr. Little's *Report on Devon, Cornwall, Dorset and Somerset*, August, 1882, pp. 6, 7.

and by members of the family, the cottager buying
roots of the farmer, and producing in return milk,
butter and pork, besides rearing calves. Among such
peasant-farmers pauperism soon ceased to exist, and
many of them soon bettered themselves in life. It
was also particularly observed that habits of market-
ing, and the constant demands on thrift and fore-
thought, brought out new virtues and powers in the
wives. In fact, the moral effects of the system in
fostering industry, sobriety, and contentment, were
described as no less satisfactory than its economical
success. On the same estate there was a regular
graduation of larger farms, ranging from those of
'one plough,' or some sixty acres up to holdings of
400*l.* a year. When a farm of 100*l.* a year fell
vacant, out of eleven eligible offers for it, four came
from promoted labourers."[1]

There remains one more point on which it is
desirable to adduce evidence, the superiority of
labourers to farmers even in wheat-growing. It has
always been denied that wheat could be well grown
on small farms, but the only evidence adduced has
been, that in France, a country of small farms, the
average produce of wheat per acre is not so high as
in England, a country of large farms. It is forgotten,
however, that if we make another comparison the
evidence is all the other way. The wheat farms in
Australia and California are far larger than in
England, but their produce per acre is very much
less. Such comparisons are really valueless, unless

[1] *English Land and English Landlords*, p. 237.

the whole conditions of farming in the countries compared are taken account of. In the case of France, for example, it has been pointed out that the reason why the wheat produce is less than with us, is because the peasant-farmers cultivate land which in England would be too poor to pay rent at all and would therefore remain waste. The supposed disadvantage of France may therefore, when the cause is understood, turn out to be a superiority.

Coming back, however, to our own country, we have some most interesting facts given us by the Rev. C. W. Stubbs, in a little book recently published, called *The Land and the Labourer.* Mr. Stubbs has some glebe at Granborough, in Buckinghamshire, which he lets out in allotments to farm-labourers at a full rent, and they grow wheat upon it. He has kept careful accounts of the yield of these allotments for nine years, with the startling result that they surpass that of the best farms in the district. His figures are as follows :—

Farmers' average in Granborough	25 bushels an acre.
Mr. Lawes' (high scientific farming) average. .	36 ,, ,,
Allotment average, Granborough	40 ,, ,,
Mr. Lawes' maximum	55 ,, ,,
Allotment maximum (W. Tomkins')	57 ,, ,,

Now here is a result of vital importance to the country, an *increase* of 15 bushels of wheat an acre *obtained by means of the spare time of labourers, which would otherwise be wasted.* If a million acres were thus cultivated, the result would be a net gain to the country of fifteen million bushels of wheat, a not unimportant addition to our national food supply, but still more important as bettering the condition of our labourers to that extent, and increasing thereby the demand for our manufactures. And this, be it remembered, under the disadvantages which have been shown to attach to mere allotments.

Notwithstanding that the many and great advantages of allowing labourers to have land under fair conditions and on a permanent tenure have been pointed out and demonstrated many times over during the last fifty years, it is still so opposed to the customs and prejudices both of landlords and farmers, that the favourable examples of it in this country may almost be counted on the fingers. Yet the benefits to be derived from the practice are of such a truly national character that it is absolutely necessary to bring it into operation over the whole country, and this can only be done by legislation which will give all classes of Englishmen (for there is no reason why the privilege should be confined to manual labourers alone) the *right* to have a plot of land to be personally occupied, and the *power* to obtain it when and where desired, at a fair rent and on a secure tenure. And this can be done without any undue interference with vested interests if we will but make the oft-repeated maxim—that property has duties as well as rights, not a mere phrase but a reality; and, now that the safety and well-being of the whole nation are seen to require it, enforce their "duty" upon landlords and give the people "rights" which have long been in abeyance.[1]

What is urgently needed is some such enactment as the following :—Any labourer who has worked on a farm, say for a year, shall have allotted to him an acre of land on that farm, at the farm rent and on a permanent tenure. If he has already a cottage on the farm, the land should be attached to the cottage; if not, he will, sooner or later, find means to get a cottage built for himself. When a man has saved money enough to stock a larger plot of land, he should be enabled to have it,. so that a race of peasant-farmers may grow up who have learnt step by step the economies and specialities of cultivation, which alone make farming successful. What has resulted in Cornwall at Penstrasse Moor, in Cheshire on Lord Tollemache's estate, on the Annandale estate in Dumfriesshire, and on Mr. Knight's estate at Exmoor, will then spread over the whole country. Our existing paupers and prospective paupers will

---

[1] Those who are still disturbed by the repeated allegations that peasant-cultivation does not succeed, are recommended to read carefully the whole of Chapters VI. and VII. of Book II. of Mill's *Political Economy*, where they will find a body of illustrative facts and weighty judgment on the subject, which, in addition to the examples here adduced, will, we believe, be held by every unprejudiced reader to be absolutely conclusive. In Chapter II., par. 6, of the same Book II. are some excellent remarks on the respective rights of landlords and of the community.

gradually be changed into industrious, thrifty, self-supporting, and self-respecting men ; our farmers will have plenty of the best of labourers upon and around their farms ; hard-working peasant - farmers will spread over the country ; land now uncultivated or half cultivated will receive that minute care and unremitting labour which is always given to it when the occupier has secure possession and the certainty of reaping all the fruits of his toil ; and food production will increase to such an extent as to add materially to the national wealth. With a general right to acquire land for personal occupation, within reasonable limits, population will flow back from the overcrowded towns to the rural districts. Our villages and hamlets, almost stationary for a century, and of late years decreasing in population, will again begin to grow. Thousands who have realised a competence will retire to live in the country when land can be had in every locality on reasonable terms. As population thus increases, and even the labourers have money to spend, there will arise openings for numerous shopkeepers, mechanics, and other workers, and many who had been obliged to leave the stagnant or decreasing villages will then gladly return to them.

And this healthy and unfettered growth of rural populations, with the improved condition of both labourers and farmers, consequent on the secure tenure of land enjoyed by both, will create a corresponding activity in our manufactures, and will tend, more quickly and more surely than anything else, to put an end to the depression of trade by that most . beneficial and effectual agency—the increased demands of a population who are yearly producing more and more wealth from the undeveloped resources of their native soil.

CHAPTER XVI.

IN pointing out the causes of the existing Depression of Trade, I placed in the foremost rank the influence of excessive Foreign Loans, because they tended, in the first place, to produce an undue inflation of our manufactures and commerce while the money was being spent—an abnormal inflation which would necessarily be followed by some degree of depression; while, secondly, by impoverishing whole nations who had to pay excessive interest on loans which had in no way benefited them, the demand for our goods was correspondingly diminished. The extent and magnitude of this cause, and its very close synchronism with the inflation and subsequent depression of our trade, appear fully to justify the place I have given it.

Next in importance comes the enormous recent increase in the armaments and general war expenditure of the great European Powers, an increase which began just before the depression manifested itself, and whose ever-increasing burden is still felt; and this, which at the same time diminishes both the production and consumption of our chief foreign customers, is an undoubted and very serious cause of depression. The two together may be considered as constituting the external element of the problem, since they chiefly affect us through our foreign trade; and taken together, I cannot doubt that they have been the most potent agent in producing the present depression.

But when we look at the problem of how to remedy the evil, the great question of the Land, in its relation to the farmer and the labourer, to the decrease of rural populations and the increase of distress and pauperism, stands far in advance of all the others, both because we hold the remedy in our own hands to apply at once, and because the remedial agency is calculated to extend far beyond the share which this particular cause has had in bringing about the present depression, and to produce beneficial results which will permanently renovate our home trade to an extent which it is almost impossible to calculate.

In order to recall to the reader's mind the magnitude and importance of this remedial agency, let me briefly summarise a few facts and conclusions. Lord Carrington's allotments produced 33l. an acre more than farms. Allotments generally have been officially estimated to produce 16l. above the farm rents, say 14l. more in produce. The Granborough allotments, cultivated in wheat, produced fifteen bushels an acre more than farms, or, at six shillings a bushel, 4l. 10s. Taking the average of these three estimates we have a nett gain of 17l. an acre above the same land cultivated, as at present, by farmers. Every one who looks about the country knows that a large proportion of our land is not half cultivated, so that the above estimates of gain by thorough peasant-culture will probably be under rather than over the mark. Now let us suppose that one half of our fifty millions of acres of farm land should be cultivated by labourers and peasant-farmers, with the result of an increased produce of 16l. an acre. That will amount to a net increase of *four hundred millions sterling a year*, produced by working men and almost all spent in home manufactures. These are the possibilities of land reform. It may take years and even generations to realise them fully, but that they may be realised, none who have carefully studied the results of peasant-culture *under the most favourable conditions*, can doubt. What we have got to do is, to see that we are put off with no half measures, but to insist, that the conditions under which labour shall have access to the soil *shall be the most favourable possible*. It is not a question of benefiting the labourers only, but through them of benefiting the whole community.

In conclusion, I wish to direct my readers' attention to a very suggestive fact elicited by our present inquiry, and which appears to me to express the moral teaching of the whole subject. In every case in which we have traced out the efficient causes of the present depression, we have found it to originate in customs, laws, or modes of action which are ethically unsound, if not positively immoral. Wars and excessive war armaments, loans to despots or for war purposes, the accumulation of vast wealth by individuals, excessive speculation, adulteration of manufactured goods, and, lastly, our bad land system, with its insecurity of tenure, excessive rents, confiscation of tenant's property, its common inclosures, evictions, and depopulation of the rural districts—all come under this category; while the one apparent exception, the bad seasons, would have been comparatively harmless (as instances here quoted have shown) under a thoroughly good system of land-tenure.

We thus see that the evils under which we have suffered, and are still suffering, are due to no recondite causes, to no laws of inevitable fluctuation of trade, but wholly to our own acts and to those of other civilised nations. Whenever we depart from the great principles of truth and honesty, of equal freedom and justice to all men whether in our relations with other states, or in our dealings with our fellow-men, the evil that we do surely comes back to us, and the suffering and poverty and crime of which we are the direct or indirect causes, help to impoverish ourselves. It is, then, by applying the teachings of a higher morality to our commerce and manufactures, to our laws and customs, and to our dealings with all other nationalities, that we shall find the only effective and permanent remedy for Depression of Trade.

THE END.

LONDON : RICHARD CLAY AND SONS, PRINTERS.

The English Citizen:

A SERIES OF SHORT BOOKS ON

HIS RIGHTS AND RESPONSIBILITIES.

EDITED BY HENRY CRAIK,

M.A. (OXON.), LL.D. (GLASGOW).

This series is intended to meet the demand for accessible information on the ordinary conditions and the current terms of our political life, and deals with the details of the machinery whereby our Constitution works, and the broad lines upon which it has been constructed.

The books are not intended to interpret disputed points in Acts of Parliament, nor to refer in detail to clauses or sections of those Acts, but to select and sum up the salient features of any branch of legislation, so as to place the ordinary citizen in possession of the main points of the law.

CENTRAL GOVERNMENT. By H. D. TRAILL, D.C.L.

THE ELECTORATE AND THE LEGISLATURE. By SPENCER WALPOLE.

THE POOR LAW. By the Rev. T. FOWLE, M.A.

THE NATIONAL BUDGET: the National Debt, Taxes, and Rates. By A. J. WILSON.

THE STATE IN RELATION TO LABOUR. By W. STANLEY JEVONS, LL.D., F.R.S.

THE STATE AND THE CHURCH. By the Hon. ARTHUR ELLIOT.

FOREIGN RELATIONS. By SPENCER WALPOLE.

THE STATE IN ITS RELATION TO TRADE. By Sir T. H. FARRER, Bart.

LOCAL GOVERNMENT. By M. D. CHALMERS, M.A.

THE STATE IN ITS RELATION TO EDUCATION. By HENRY CRAIK, M.A., LL.D.

THE LAND LAWS. By Professor F. POLLOCK.

COLONIES AND DEPENDENCIES:—
PART I.—INDIA. By J. S. COTTON, M.A.
„ II.—THE COLONIES. By E. J. PAYNE, M.A.

JUSTICE AND POLICE. By F. W. MAITLAND.

THE PUNISHMENT AND PREVENTION OF CRIME. By Sir EDMUND DU CANE, K.C.B.

THE NATIONAL DEFENCES. By Colonel MAURICE, R.A. [*In preparation.*

MACMILLAN AND CO., LONDON.

www.ingramcontent.com/pod-product-compliance
Lightning Source LLC
Chambersburg PA
CBHW020751020726
47495CB00008B/2380

* 9 7 8 3 3 3 7 4 0 0 1 8 7 *